Childcraft
ANIMAL FRIENDS AND ADVENTURES

MILO WINTER

Childcraft

IN FIFTEEN VOLUMES

•

VOLUME FOUR

ANIMAL FRIENDS AND ADVENTURES

FIELD ENTERPRISES EDUCATIONAL CORPORATION
Merchandise Mart Plaza · Chicago 54, Illinois

Printed in the United States of America

EIA

CONTENTS

ANIMAL FRIENDS

WHEELS, WINGS, AND REAL THINGS

ACKNOWLEDGMENTS

The publishers of CHILDCRAFT gratefully acknowledge the courtesy of the following publishers for permission to use the following copyrighted stories, poems, and illustrations:

Child Life magazine and the authors for the following:

"Wappie's Surprise Cake" by Harriet Bunn; "Dandi, the Deer" by Belle Coates; "All Aboard the De Witt Clinton!" by Jeannette Covert Nolan; "Steam Comes Upriver" by Josephine E. Phillips; "Freddie the Great" by Ruth Cromer Weir.

Doubleday & Company, Inc.: "How the Camel Got His Hump" from *Just So Stories* by Rudyard Kipling, copyright 1912, 1897. Courtesy A. P. Watt & Co.; The Macmillan Co. of Canada; and Messrs. Macmillan & Co., Ltd.

Follet Publishing Company: "The Pulling Bee" from *Justin Morgan Had a Horse* by Marguerite Henry.

Greenberg, Publisher: "The Last of the Dragons" from *Five of Us—And Madeline.* Courtesy John Farquharson of London.

Harcourt, Brace & Company, Inc.: "A Miserable Merry Christmas" from *Boy on Horseback* by Lincoln Steffens, copyright 1931, 1935, by Harcourt, Brace & Company, Inc.

Houghton Mifflin Company: "Three Boys on the Subway" from *Sad-Faced Boy* by Arna Bontemps.

J. Morris Jones: "The Little Old Truck" by J. Morris Jones.

J. B. Lippincott Company: "Uncle Harry and the Aunts" from *Father's Big Improvements* by Caroline D. Emerson.

Estate of Hugh Lofting: "Doctor Dolittle's Pushmi-Pullyu" from *The Story of Doctor Dolittle* by Hugh Lofting.

The Macmillan Company: "Bidushka Lays an Easter Egg" from *Maminka's Children* by Elizabeth Orton Jones; "The Cub and the Crocodile" from *The Lion-Hearted Kitten and Other Stories* by Peggy Bacon; "A Bird Cage with Tassels" from *The Dream Coach* by Ann Parrish; "A Rare Provider" from *Magical Melons* by Carol Ryrie Brink; "Six Days on an Ocean Liner" from *Full Steam Ahead* by Henry B. Lent.

Oxford University Press: "Johnny and His Mule" by Ellis Credle, copyright 1946 by Oxford University Press.

Row, Peterson & Company: "When a Modern Boy Travels" from *Land Travel* by Frances Cavanah, copyright 1942 by Row, Peterson & Company.

Charles Scribner's Sons: "The Family Who Had Never Had Roller Skates" from *Time Was* by Hildegard Woodward, copyright 1941 by Charles Scribner's Sons; "A Little Black Bear Goes to School" from *The School Bell Rings* by Evelyn Ray Sickels, copyright 1942 by Charles Scribner's Sons; "Christopher" by Marjorie Flack from *Stories for Fun* by Charlotte Becker, copyright 1941 by Charles Scribner's Sons.

State Publishing House, Prague: "Hare's Birthday Party" from *Forest Story* by Josef Kozisek.

Story Parade, Inc.: "Meals for Mickey" by Alice Dalgleish, copyright 1947 by Story Parade, Inc.

Albert Whitman & Company: "Timmy Rides the China Clipper" adapted from *Timmy Rides the China Clipper* by Carol Nay.

ANIMAL FRIENDS

*Bunny the Brave**

By Dhan Gopal Mukerji

ONE day, the King of a jungle, the Elephant, said to his subjects, "Summer is ending; there has been a lot of rain now. The grass and the leaves are plentiful. Now I do not need to be busy all the time looking after your food supply, my subjects. And since I need a little rest, I shall leave you all for a month and go to the seashore."

Of course his subjects, the cows, the deer, the boars, the antelopes, the monkeys, and the rabbits felt sad at his going. But since they realized that their King was good and kind, and since he had been working very hard of late, he had better go on a month's vacation. So the Elephant, tall as a housetop and big as a cathedral, swung out of his jungle, and pretty soon vanished out of sight like a vast black cloud lost in the silver spaces of the evening sky.

His subjects, though somewhat dejected by his going away, in a couple of days pulled themselves together and set to work.

*Taken from *Hindu Fables for Little Children* by Dhan Gopal Mukerji, published by E. P. Dutton & Company, Inc., copyright 1929.

BUNNY THE BRAVE

Now that the leaves burned like opulent torches of green, and the grass that trammeled their feet tasted lush and thick, they set to work to pile up their store for the winter, which would be upon them soon enough.

In the jungle you stock up things just when the heavy rain has fallen and the big rivers and the little rivers are so full that they can hardly sing.

Regarding work, there are two laws of work in the jungle. One is that all grownups do useful and hard work. The other law is that the young must not work in holes in the ground, nor should they do heavy work on the ground. They are employed in running errands most of the time. There was one youngster in this jungle who was just the right person. He was little Bunny, the youngest of the rabbit household. He was called little, in spite of his big healthy body. While the grownups worked, he sang songs and danced all manner of dances to amuse them. This he did when he was not running errands. Bunny was called the soul of any party. They never gave a party without asking him.

One day, as the sun was setting, the jungle folks stopped work. They asked Bunny to dance for them. Just think of the golden gloom of the evening swiftly coming upon them, and crickets and other grass-dwellers singing from the floor of the forest. From the treetops the purple, the blue, and the yellow and red birds sang trill upon trill, cadenza upon cadenza, till the entire jungle grew truly into a theater of a thousand sweet sounds and scenes. Bunny was dancing a wonderful jig to the music of birds and insects.

But, lo! Suddenly everything stopped. The entire jungle was still like a frightened child. The cows looked at the deer in surprise. The deer, in utter amazement,

looked at the family of boars. Why? Who was this? What does it all mean? Before them they saw Bunny slink away to his parents, and in his place—a big Tiger. The old fellow opened his mouth full of teeth sharp as knives, then roared. This he did thrice, as if to clear his throat.

Then he said, in a mean, hard voice, "I see that you have no king in your jungle. I was passing by when I saw that stupid Bunny dance."

This made Bunny angry. But he controlled himself, as all good young people should. The tiger went on, "I think you need a king, for there is no king here. So I shall be your king from now on."

To that remark all the animals protested. Even the insects chirped their protest. "Yao-yawoo!" roared the tiger. "Enough," he said, "I am your king now. I will kill the lot of you if you protest again. Now listen to me. I shall make my home here. Since I am of a superior race, I eat no grass or leaves, as you do. I eat meat. So send me one member—the youngest one—from each family for each day. Tomorrow send me a rabbit from the rabbit family. Day after, send me a deer from the deer family. So on, and so on, as long as I live. Now go home, every one of you. Obey your king. Don't forget to send me that rabbit for my dinner."

Now the poor sweet peaceful jungle folks went to their respective homes, their hearts heavy with pain and their heads full of the thoughts of the morrow.

At last the next day came, when Bunny had to be sent to Mr. Tiger to be his dinner. It was just the day before the old King Elephant was expected to be back. Though all their hearts were woe-laden, the animals rejoiced at the thought that in another day's time their master and friend would come back and gore that loathsome tiger with his tusks, which were as long as a man is tall.

Just the same, everybody felt sad, Bunny's parents in particular. They just could not let Bunny go. But he was so brave that he did not shed a tear, nor did he allow his parents to cry. He sang and whistled as he left home at midday.

Instead of going to Mr. Tiger's at once, he loafed and loitered on his way. About one hour later, he came across a deep, deep well, way down in the ground. As he crept to its side and looked, he saw another rabbit there. Of course he, being clever, knew that water is like a mirror: in it you can see your own face. Bunny looked at himself in that well very carefully. He also noticed that the water was so far below that it looked like the end of everything. He said to himself, "If I fall there, I shall fall so far and so deep that it will kill me at once." With those words he crept away from the edge of the well. But just before he had quite done so, he whistled. Lo, from the well the echo of his whistling came back exactly as if another bunny were whistling from way down there.

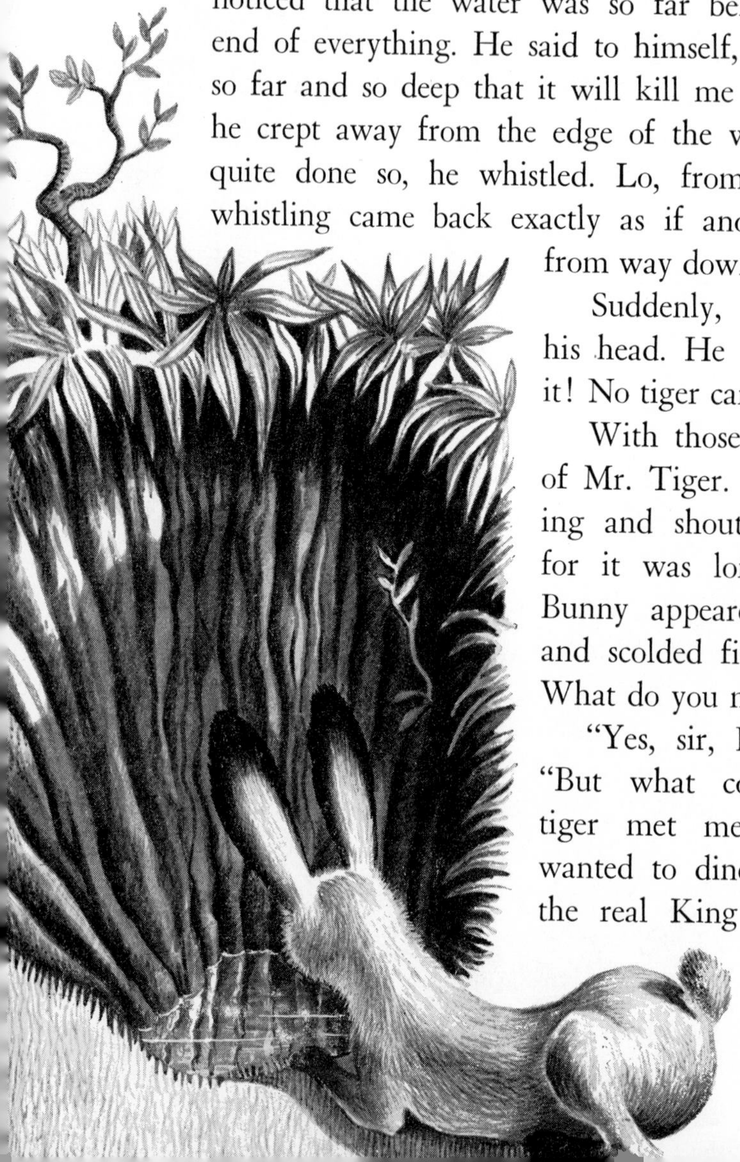

Suddenly, a strange idea came into his head. He shouted, "I have it—I have it! No tiger can eat me now!"

With those words he ran to the house of Mr. Tiger. There Mr. Tiger was, yelling and shouting. He was very hungry, for it was long past dinnertime. When Bunny appeared before him, he snarled and scolded fiercely. "Why are you late? What do you mean? Do you know that—"

"Yes, sir, I know," answered Bunny. "But what could I do when another tiger met me on my way here, and wanted to dine on me, saying that he is the real King of our jungle—not you."

"Who? How? What!" exclaimed Mr. Tiger, in amazement.

"Yes, sir. It was he who delayed me. He has sent me here to ask you to meet him," added Bunny.

"Meet him!" growled Mr. Tiger. "I shall meet him in single combat and kill him. After that, I shall eat you. Now show me the impostor."

"Thank you, sir," answered Bunny. "Now will you be kind enough to let me go ahead of you, sir, and lead you to him?"

"Get on, get on," snarled Mr. Tiger. The brute never noticed what a well-bred person Bunny was.

Bunny went on and on, as if he were on a road that had no end. Every now and then he nibbled at some grass. He needed food all right. But the wretched tiger, who ate only meat, did not eat any grass. So he grew hungrier, and more and more tired. He yelled, he grumbled, then swore, which was very rude. But Bunny was such a gentleman that he never stooped to notice Mr. Tiger's ill-bred remarks.

At last, unable to bear with it any longer, the monster shouted, "Where is that other tiger? If you don't produce him in five minutes, I will gobble you up."

"If you please, sir," answered Bunny, "he is right there, sir. Do you see that hole in the ground ahead? That is his home, dear Mr. Tiger."

"Don't you call me 'dear Mr. Tiger!'" With that rebuke, Mr. Tiger leaped right ahead. Lo and behold! Sure enough, he saw another tiger in that hole in the ground—but that hole was so deep, way, way down in the ground.

Bunny stood about six yards away from that hole. He knew that it was the old well. He also knew that the tiger was looking at his own self in the mirror of the water below.

But tigers are cruel, and therefore stupid. So, instead of thinking the thing out, Mr. Tiger, the moment he saw his own face down in that well, shouted, "You rascally tiger, you say that you are the King of this jungle! I say you are not. I will kill you!" He really thought he was talking to another tiger.

Of course, the echo came up from way below, shouting the self-same challenge at him, "You rascally tiger. You say that you are the King of this jungle! I say you are not. I will kill you!"

The tiger yelled again, "Do you dare mimic me?" The echo shouted back at him, "Do you dare mimic me?"

Mr. Tiger shouted anew, "You coward, I will kill you where you are!" Then he jumped! Lo, instead of coming upon another tiger, he fell through a long empty hole into a deep, deep body of water, which had hardly any bottom at all, it was so deep.

Now that he had succeeded in killing Mr. Tiger by letting him drown himself in that well, Bunny went home.

He reached home just at sunset. His parents were so surprised to find him alive, that they could hardly believe their eyes. Tears of joy danced in them. Mother Rabbit said, "Where is the tiger?"

Bunny answered, "I killed him!"

His mother said, "You are joking."

But Bunny said, "Come with me, and I shall show you."

It was true that the tiger was dead and afloat in the well. When the King Elephant returned the next day, he christened the little rabbit "Bunny the Brave."

From *Hindu Fables*

Hare's Birthday Party

By Josef Kozisek

HARE loved his home, and really, he had a right to. He had the coziest little house built under the wild brier bush on the edge of the poppy and cyclamen meadow. Such a convenient place! When Fox came sniffing along, the tall meadow grasses hid Hare's escape. When Buzzard circled above him, the convenient forest sheltered him. When Owl hunted him in the forest, a few great leaps took him under the bramble bush, where he lay like a length of shadow. Above all, when he felt like an outing with his friends, he could reach the clearing in half a dozen great hops.

Hare loved his friends, and his friends loved Hare. They went to him for everything. He always seemed to know just what to say and do, though there were times when Hare loved to play a good joke on them all.

One morning, on his birthday, he called the bird concert troupe together and told them to be ready to entertain, for he was going to have a surprise party for his friends. He didn't wish to bother them with present-bringing, but he had managed to arrange to have them all come, one after the other, to see him.

Even as he was speaking, Rabbit was scurrying along, wondering what Hare wished to ask of him.

As Rabbit passed the mushroom circle, he heard a shrill crying. Surely that was Mouse! He peeped under a toadstool, and there he saw her, the bright tears running down her sharp little gray nose.

"Little Friend Mouse, why do you weep?" asked Rabbit.

"I weep because of my loss," cried Mouse. "Yesterday my sister Long Tail walked with me among the mushrooms, but today I walk alone. She went out before me this morning, and I have looked everywhere for her. I know Owl has eaten her up by this time."

"Perhaps yes, perhaps no," said Rabbit. "Two are better than one. We'll search for her together."

They walked on until they came to Squirrel, crying into her handkerchief.

"Little Friend Squirrel, why do you weep?" asked Rabbit.

"I weep because of my loss," cried Squirrel. "Yesterday my sister Quick Feet ran with me through the nut trees, but today I run alone. She went out before me this morning, and I have looked everywhere for her. I know Buzzard has eaten her up by this time!"

"Perhaps yes, perhaps no," said Rabbit. "Three are better than two, and two are better than one. We'll search for her and Long Tail together."

The three walked on until they came to Badger, wiping his eyes with his clumsy paws.

HARE'S BIRTHDAY PARTY

"Big Friend Badger, why do you weep?" asked Rabbit.

"I weep because of my loss," cried Badger. "Yesterday my Lady Badger nibbled with me among the green twigs, but today I nibble alone. She went out before me this morning, and I have looked everywhere for her. I know Wolf has eaten her up by this time."

"Perhaps yes, perhaps no," said Rabbit. "Four are better than three; three are better than two; two are better than one. We'll search for her and Quick Feet and Long Tail together."

The four walked on till they met Hedgehog, who was carrying a great basketful of things. Rabbit spied a bunch of carrots, and at once burst into tears. The animals all stared at him, amazed.

"Little Friend Rabbit, why do *you* weep?" they all asked.

"I weep because of my loss," cried Rabbit. "Yesterday my brother Bunny rooted carrots with me in the garden, but today I root carrots alone. He went out before me this morning, and I forgot all about him, for I was on my way to Hare's to see what he wanted of me. When I saw those carrots, I remembered that he left early. I know Fox has eaten him by this time."

"Perhaps yes, perhaps no," chuckled Hedgehog. "Five are better than four; four are better than three; three are better than two; two are better than one. Let's search for them all together. But first, let's stop in and see Hare a minute. It's his birthday, and I've some fine presents for him."

The animals dried their eyes, and Hedgehog went on, "Rabbit, just take this cabbage. Mouse, you gather some four-leaf clovers to wish him good luck. Squirrel, you bring a nice bouquet of cyclamens and poppies. Badger, bring a lettuce from my garden. I've this big bunch of carrots. We'll congratulate Hare first, give him our fine gifts, and then ask him about our lost friends. Come."

When they came near the brier patch, there they saw Hare sitting before his door, smoking sweetgrass. Little Friend Mouse was the first to greet him, and he looked so friendly she burst out crying as she handed him the four-leaf clovers.

"Take these for luck," she cried. "May you never be eaten up by Owl as Sister Long Tail was this morning, when I was too lazy to hurry out with her."

HARE'S BIRTHDAY PARTY

"Oh, good Friend Hare," wept Squirrel, "take these flowers with my best wishes. May you never have to gather more in memory of some loved one, as I must do this very day for Sister Quick Feet, who has been eaten up by Buzzard, and all because I stole her nuts last night."

"Here's a lettuce, green and tender," sniffed clumsy Badger. "May you live to share many with Lady Hare, as I may never again hope to share one with Lady Badger, who has been eaten by Wolf, all because I wouldn't share green twigs with her."

Then up stepped poor little Rabbit, trying to be brave, but sniffing for all that. "Nice Uncle Hare," he said, "here's a wonderful cabbage for your birthday. May you divide it with all my little cousins as I may never divide one with my brother. He has been eaten by Fox, I know, and I never even missed him till I met Hedgehog."

"Neighbor Hare," chuckled old Hedgehog, winking slyly, "here are carrots enough for four and four and a dozen more. Perhaps, in exchange, you can help to make us merry."

"Perhaps I can," laughed Hare, and twitched his left ear at an oriole sitting above him. Immediately the bird concert tuned up. As the merry melodies filled the bramblebush cottage, its door swung open wide, and the five visitors looked in to see a wondrous birthday feast spread upon a snowy cloth. But more wondrous still were the merry guests, for with Wife Hare were Lady Badger, Brother Bunny, Long Tail, and Quick Feet. Hedgehog and Hare shook with laughter at the joke played by Hare, but Mouse, Squirrel, Badger, and Rabbit looked a bit ashamed as they slipped into the empty chairs about the table.

As soon as Hare took his place at the head of the table, however, and, holding a four-leaf clover in his hand, wished them all luck for the rest of the year, they fell to giggling and joking and eating with never a memory of sigh or tear.

HARE'S BIRTHDAY PARTY

At last Hedgehog sprang to his feet and cried out, "Hurrah for Neighbor Hare, who has made us remember certain things we owe our families. And hurrah for our families, who would rather find each other than all the birthday presents in the world."

"Hurrah for friend Hedgehog," answered Hare modestly. "If we had to get along without that gallant knight, where would we be? Fox, Buzzard, Owl, Wolf; he protects us from them all."

"Hurrah for Hedgehog and Hare," they all shouted.

"And for birthdays," squeaked Mouse.

"And for birthday parties," squealed Squirrel.

"Hurrah for everything and all of us," whispered the tiny wee brother Bunny. And with that they ended the feast of the Hare's birthday party.

From *A Forest Story*

R. B.

Christopher

By Marjorie Flack

ONCE upon a time there were four very small puppies who lived in a basket with their mother.

Now one of these puppies was much larger and much stronger than any of the other puppies.

He was so much larger and so much stronger than the others, that, while they could only crawl around on their tummies, he could stand up on his four fat little legs.

One day this large puppy put his front paws up over the side of the basket and he wiggled and wiggled, until, flop, there he was outside the basket! Then off he wobbled to see what he could find.

So he was named Christopher, for Christopher Columbus, because he was such a brave explorer.

When Christopher grew larger, he did not live in the basket any more. He lived in a house with a girl named Sally and a boy named Tom. The larger Christopher grew, the more he liked exploring.

Christopher liked to explore the molehills, and around trees, and under the kitchen porch, and in the brook, and many other places just to see what he could find.

But most of all he liked to go exploring with Sally and Tom in the car.

Sometimes they would stop at the grocery shop and Christopher would find a cat to tease.

Sometimes they would stop at the butcher shop and Christopher would find a bone. Sometimes, best of all, they would stop at Grandmother's house and they would all find cookies there.

One Sunday morning when Christopher was exploring the garden, he heard Sally calling, "Here, Christopher! Here, Christopher!"

And he heard Tom calling, "Here, Christopher, come here, Christopher!"

So Christopher ran into the house to see why they wanted him.

"We are going in the car to Grandmother's house this afternoon," said Tom.

When Christopher heard the word, "car," he wagged his tail and barked with joy.

"And we are going to give you a nice bath now, so you will be all beautiful and clean when you go with us," said Sally.

When Christopher heard the word, "bath," he stopped wagging his tail and he stopped barking for joy; and he ran upstairs and he hid under the bed. Christopher hid because he did not like baths.

But Sally pulled him out, and then she held him in the tub while Tom scrubbed him. Then Tom held him while Sally scrubbed him, and then they rinsed Christopher. They rinsed him in bluing water until he was as white as snow. Then they rubbed him and tied him up in a towel and put him in the sun in the kitchen to dry.

"Now," said Sally, "you are a beautiful clean Christopher!"

"Lie down," said Tom, "and stay there

until you are dry."

Then Sally and Tom went away, and Christopher was left alone in the sun in the kitchen to dry.

But Christopher did not stay there. He saw a squirrel outside the window, so he pushed open the screen door. Out he ran, towel and all.

But up the squirrel ran, up high in the tree.

So Christopher went exploring under the porch, around the trees, in the brook and mole-hills, until he was no longer white as snow.

Then Christopher saw a rabbit looking at him from under a bush. Quickly Christopher dashed over the ground. Quickly he scrambled under the bush, but—he stopped. Christopher stopped because he was caught by the towel in the bush!

Christopher saw the squirrel jumping from tree to tree. He tried to go this way, and he tried to go that way. The more he tried to get away the more Christopher got tangled up in the bush. There was nothing for him to do but wait.

Christopher saw the squirrel jumping from tree to tree. He saw the rabbit hopping about. He saw a mouse come running out.

But poor Christopher could not chase them, he could not move, he could only wait. He waited and waited until at last he heard Sally calling, "Here, Christopher, here, Christopher!" And he heard Tom calling, "Here, Christopher! Come here, Christopher!"

But Christopher could not go to them, because he was tangled in the bush.

So he called to them. He called, "YIP — YIPPPPPP-YIP."

At last he saw them come running to him, and Sally said, "Naughty Christopher, you naughty Christopher. Look, you are all muddy and dirty!"

And Tom said, "We'll have to give you a bath all over again."

So Sally and Tom untangled Christopher from the bush, and they took him home, and they gave him a bath all over again. They scrubbed him and they rinsed him in bluing water, and they rubbed him and they wrapped him in another towel and put him in the kitchen to dry.

"Now," said Tom, "stay there. Stay there until you are all nice and dry, so you can go with us in the car to Grandmother's house."

So Sally and Tom went away, and soon Christopher saw the squirrel outside the window. He saw the rabbit looking out from the bush. He saw the field mouse come running out.

But he stayed there. Christopher stayed right there in the sun in the kitchen to dry. So, when Tom and Sally were all ready to go, there was Christopher all nice and dry and as clean and as white as snow!

So Christopher and Sally and Tom all rode away in the car to Grandmother's house to see what they could find.

From *Stories for Fun*

The Cub and the Crocodile

By Peggy Bacon

ONCE there was a baby crocodile who lay in the shallow water at the edge of a broad river, pretending he was nothing but a log of wood. His careful mother had taught him how to look like a log of wood, so he was doing it very well indeed, although he was still so young. His back was round and rough and dark like the wet bark of a log; his feet were buried in the mud of the river bank, and he kept his rows of sharp white teeth well under the water where they could not be seen.

Along came a lion cub who had run away from his mother because she wanted to wash his face. He did not enjoy having his face washed, so while she turned to wash the face of one of his brothers, he slipped out of the cave where they all lived together, and made for the river.

When he reached the riverside he stopped, looked across the water, and thought to himself how green and pretty everything was on the other side. It appeared to be nicer over there than on the side where he stood, though really it was much the same. "I should like to play all afternoon in those cool woods far from Mother, who washes my face," said he. "If I go back now she will spank me for running away, but if I am gone all afternoon she will be frightened. Then when I return at suppertime she will be so glad to see me safe at home that she will give me a kiss instead of a spanking. How can I cross the river?"

Right in the middle of the stream was a large rock; from the opposite bank onto this rock had fallen a tall tree, along which he might easily walk to shore. And directly in front of him lay what he thought to be a floating log of wood. If he were to step on the log, and creep carefully to the other end, perhaps he would be able to leap as far as the big rock. So out he stepped.

To his surprise he immediately discovered that he was not stepping on a log of wood at all, but on a small crocodile who lifted up his head with a cross look and snapped his teeth together in a very naughty way.

"Good gracious, pardon me!" exclaimed the cub, jumping quickly back to the bank. The baby crocodile had nearly snapped off the fluffy end of his tail. The lion cub sat down on the moss and stared at the baby crocodile.

"*Where* do you think you are going, and *who* do you think I am?" snarled the crocodile. His mother had taught him to speak always with rudeness and ferocity, because crocodiles believe it safe and proper to behave that way. The baby crocodile was really a gentle little beast, but he did his best to appear dangerous.

The lion cub, however, was not deceived. He saw a creature no larger than himself, but with much shorter legs and a long, cumbersome tail. It was apparently stuck fast in the mud. So, though he was rather dazzled by the long rows of sharp white teeth, he spoke up bravely and politely as his mother had taught him to do—for lions believe it wise to be courteous and dignified, even in emergencies.

"I wish to get across the stream," he

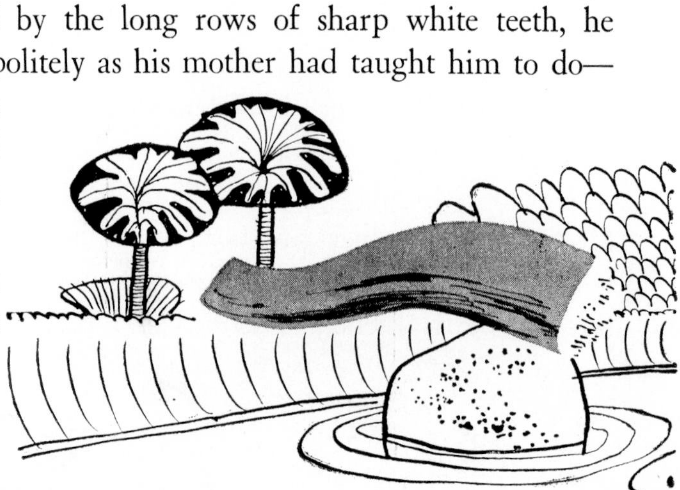

answered, "and I thought you were a log of wood. I hope that I did not frighten you by jumping on your back so suddenly," he added.

The baby crocodile blinked his eyes in wonder; he had tried hard to look like a log of wood and had expected to scare the wits out of the lion cub. He forgot to be cross and smiled pleasantly.

"Get on my back and I will carry you as far as the rock," he said to the cub, who promptly did as he was bid and was carried over the water.

"Tell me," queried the crocodile curiously, "what do you expect to find on the other side?"

"I do not know," replied the cub, "but I am sure there must be many things to see and I would like to explore all afternoon. Will you be so good as to carry me back again after a while?"

"Maybe," replied the crocodile, remembering just in time that his mother had told him never to say "yes." However, he remained by the rock, waiting.

The lion cub thanked the crocodile, trotted along the fallen tree, and gained the bank. He wandered through the woods, discovering to his surprise that things were nearly the same on this side of the river as on the side from which he had come. The trees were no taller, the grass and ferns no greener; the same sort of berries grew upon the bushes, and the same kinds of little creatures came out to look at him. The only difference was that as the sun began to sink he felt a certain fear growing inside him, for he knew that his mother and father were not here to look out for him, but far away on the other side of the water. The woods grew strange and hushed; everything was quiet, and the path unfamiliar. The cub began to be afraid and turned to go home, when suddenly from the bushes beside him came a dreadful hiss, and the biggest, wickedest snake he had ever seen lifted its head out of the leaves.

The cub did not wait to fluff his tail or hiss back at the snake; he just turned and ran as fast as he could back to the river, the wicked snake behind him. The snake would have caught him, but the cub jumped onto the back of the baby crocodile who carried him quickly across the stream.

When they reached the other side the lion cub was still so frightened that words failed him. He was so frightened he didn't know what to say to show how grateful he was to the crocodile.

THE CUB AND THE CROCODILE

All he uttered was, "Thank you, thank you, thank you," but his eyes showed how he felt.

"Pooh, that's nothing," replied the baby crocodile, with suitable gruffness, but he smiled in the most friendly way.

The lion cub crept home to the cave and snuggled against his mother who, as he had expected, did not spank him. She kissed him and then she washed his face, but this time he did not mind.

Later on, when his brothers and sisters lost their first teeth, the cub collected them as they dropped out and strung them into a lovely necklace, which he presented with a pretty speech to his little crony, the crocodile.

"Teeth!" snapped the latter sharply, "I have enough teeth." But he always wore the necklace.

From *The Lion-Hearted Kitten and Other Stories*

*Mrs. Goose's Wild Christmas**

By Miriam Clark Potter

ONE morning in December when Mrs. Goose went to her front door, there was a letter for her. It was written on birchbark paper and tied around with green grass ribbon.

Mrs. Goose was so excited that her wings fluttered and trembled. She opened the envelope, sat down in her little rocking chair, and put on her glasses.

The letter was printed in queer, green, wiggly letters. It said:

"Dear Mrs. Goose,

Please come and spend Christmas with me in my river home. I will fly by for you at five o'clock on Christmas Eve. Be ready to fly up and fly away with me.

Your flying cousin,
Mrs. Wild-Goose-of-the-Marshes."

"My, there are a lot of 'flys' in that letter," said Mrs. Goose, blinking. She got up from her rocking chair and said to herself, "I don't believe I know how to fly. I've been a tame goose for so long that I've forgotten."

She thought for a minute, and then she flapped her wings. "No, I haven't forgotten," she told herself.

Three-Ducks were coming over for a cup of hot clover tea at four o'clock. Mrs. Goose kept very busy till they came, tying up presents for her friends. She had three yellow bow ties for Three-

Ducks, a nice new tail comb for Mrs. Squirrel, and currant cakes for Mr. Pig and the Pop-Rabbits and her other friends. "Don't open till Christmas," she wrote on them.

"My friends can look at them when they have the big Animaltown Christmas Tree party," she planned. "But I won't be here!" Yes, she had decided to spend Christmas with her wild marsh cousin.

At four o'clock, she heard a quacking at the door, and she ran to let Three-Ducks in. "It's getting very cold and blowy," they told her, as they marched over to the fire. "We think it's going to snow," they said, as they warmed their wings.

"I hope it won't snow on Christmas Eve at five o'clock," Mrs. Goose told them, "because I am going away then."

"Away?" quacked Three-Ducks, looking at her.

"Yes, away; I am going to visit my cousin, Mrs. Wild-Goose," and she showed them the birchbark letter.

"Oh, Mrs. Goose, you won't be here for Christmas and our big Animaltown party," said Three-Ducks.

"No."

"Why, we'll miss you so much!"

"I'll miss you, too," said Mrs. Goose, getting the teapot.

"And you'll not like the way your cousin lives. She doesn't have a cozy home like yours! She sleeps in a wet river place."

Mrs. Goose poured the tea. "Yes, but she *is* my cousin," she told Three-Ducks. "Our mothers were sister geese. I have decided to go."

They drank their tea, and they talked some more about it, but

Three-Ducks couldn't make Mrs. Goose change her mind. She was just determined to go on Christmas Eve.

On the day before Christmas, Mrs. Goose was very busy. She tied bright bunches of holly berries on her friends' presents. She packed a little bag with her long gray nightgown and white nightcap and feather-brush. She swept her house and put it all in order. Then she put on her red shoes and her blue and lavender dress and bright red shawl and hat with parsley on it.

She looked at herself in the glass and said, "There I am. I look very handsome, really—I hope my cousin will be proud of me."

Tap--tap—tap. There were Three-Ducks at the door. They had come to see her off. *Scratch—scratch—scratch.* That was Mrs. Squirrel. Then came Mr. Pig and Mr. Gobbler and the Pop-Rabbits. It was very exciting—just like waiting to see a balloon go up, or something. "Do you *know* how to fly?" asked Mrs. Squirrel. "Yes, I know," answered Mrs. Goose.

They all went outside to watch for Mrs. Wild-Goose.

The wind made little scurry-tracks in the snow, and there were gray clouds scudding over. "I wish she'd hurry," said Mrs. Goose, drawing her shawl closer around her. "I'm cold."

"I wish you'd change your mind," sighed Mrs. Squirrel. "I hate to think of your flying around loose in the sky. Don't go!!"

"Yes, I'm going," said Mrs. Goose, firmly.

"I don't believe her cousin is coming," Three-Ducks whispered. "It's five minutes past five already."

But just then there was a faraway honking sound. In a minute, a wild goose came into sight. She came nearer and nearer. She flew right over Mrs. Goose's chimney.

"There she is! Good-by," said Mrs. Goose, flapping her wings.

But there she stayed, right on the ground.

"Try again," said Three-Ducks.

She flapped and flapped, but she did not rise.

"Take off your clothes!" came a wild voice from the sky. "Throw off your bag! You are too-o-o heavy!" And there was a sound like laughter, cold laughter, with wind in it.

So Mrs. Goose took off her dress and her shawl and her hat, and threw her bag down on the ground. She flapped her wings again, and up she rose, with a great noise. As she rose, she kicked off her red shoes. They fell and one whacked Mr. Pig on the nose.

"Good-by, Mrs. Goose," Mr. Pig sneezed.

"Good-by," they all called.

"Good-by," she answered them, as she rose higher and higher.

"There she goes, for her wild Christmas," said Three-Ducks. "I hope she'll have a good time." They gulped hard in their throats, because they missed her already. "We'd better take her things into the house, and lock the door, just as she told us to, and put the key under the mat. There she flies—over the pine treetops. There are going to be lots of presents for her at the Christmas party tomorrow—and she won't be here to get them. She said she'd open them when she got back."

"Maybe she won't *get* back," sighed Mrs. Squirrel. "Maybe we'll never see her again." And they all began to cry a little, feeling so sad on Christmas Eve at quarter past five o'clock.

At seven o'clock, when Three-Ducks came back from visiting

Mrs. Squirrel, there was a light shining from Mrs. Goose's window.

"We must go and look in," they said. "Who could be there? Mrs. Goose is away. We must go and see."

So they plopped over and peeked in the window.

There was Mrs. Goose with her wrapper and white nightcap on, warming her wings before the fire.

Tap—tap—tap at the door went Three-Ducks, with excited bills. They were *so* glad!

"Shhhhhh!" said Mrs. Goose, as she let them in. "Yes, I'm back. (Whisper.) Yes, my wings are tired. (*Please* whisper!) For my wild cousin is here—she's in my bed, sleeping. She's come to spend Christmas with me."

"But we thought you were going to spend Christmas with *her!"*

"I did spend two hours with her," said Mrs. Goose. "That was long enough. Yes, you were right, Three-Ducks. Her house is very cold. Just frozen rattly reeds, lumps of ice, and wind blowing your feathers this way and that. One of my best tail feathers blew right out! She had a few wintergreen berries stuck around; we ate those. 'This is our Christmas dinner, really,' said my cousin. 'We'll have it today, instead of tomorrow. We'll spend Christmas flying, my tame cousin. You need practice. You fly very badly. We'll go far over those snow-covered hills.' "

MRS. GOOSE'S WILD CHRISTMAS

"How cold and unpleasant," shivered Three-Ducks. "What did you say?"

"I said, 'Now I've had a sort of Christmas with you—a nice berry meal. Please come back to my house with me, and see what Christmas there is like. We give presents to each other; we have a party and lots of dancing and laughing, and try to make each other happy and full of pleasant feelings.' And do you know—she had never heard of a party in a house beside a fire? She didn't know about giving presents! Awfully wild, I think. Well, I talked and talked, and after a while she said she would come."

"And she's here now—sleeping in your bed?" asked Three-Ducks. "Oh, do let us have a peek at her, please."

"Will you be very quiet? Will you put your feet down softly, and not quack?"

"Oh, yes; yes."

So Mrs. Goose lit a candle, and they stepped softly to the bedroom. She held the light up high, so they could see better.

But there was no one in the bed!

The covers were thrown back, as though someone had got out quickly, and there was one long feather on the blanket.

"Why, she's *gone,*" said Mrs. Goose, looking at the open window.

"She's flown away. You can't

be wild, and she can't be tame," said Three-Ducks, wisely.

"Our mothers were sister geese," Mrs. Goose told them. "But *we* don't seem to belong in the same family."

"And you'll be here for the Christmas party, after all," laughed Three-Ducks.

* * * * *

And they had the happiest Christmas that they had ever had. Ragtag and Bobtail and Billy Squirrel and all the other animal children had some toys, and all the grown-up animals had great fun opening their own presents. They sang animal songs, and played games, and the refreshments were delicious. The tree was trimmed with balls of cotton, strings of pink popcorn, and a few stars and candles.

Mrs. Goose was so happy that she got all mixed up. She dropped nuts into her tea instead of lemon, said "Happy Birthday" to Mr. Pig instead of "Merry Christmas," and when it was time to go home, she put her rubbers on her wings instead of on her feet. But no one cared, they were so glad to see her back again. "And you won't fly away again, will you?" Three-Ducks asked her.

And she said, "No. One wild Christmas is enough for me. Animaltown is where *I* belong, forever and ever!"

From *Mrs. Goose and Three-Ducks*

Bidushka Lays an Easter Egg

By Elizabeth Orton Jones

EARLY in the morning the great green rooster crowed—
Rooka-roodle-oo!

Then a little sparrow cheeped. Old Horse stamped his foot in the barn. Old Cow swished some hay. It was the day before Easter!

Marianka got up to feed her chickens. She put on her clothes, tied her little red shawl over her head, and tiptoed down the stairs to the kitchen. She filled a bowl with chicken feed and slipped a long red apple peeling, a lovely blue prune, a bright green pepper, a light green cabbage leaf, a purple beet, and some white, white rice into her pocket. Then she went out past the barn to a place where the ground was bare.

"Come, chick-chick-chick-chick!" called Marianka, very softly, as she sprinkled chicken feed. "Come, chick-chick-chick!"

And her chickens came.

Now Marianka's red hen laid little brown eggs, and her white hen laid little white ones. But her big speckled Bidushka laid

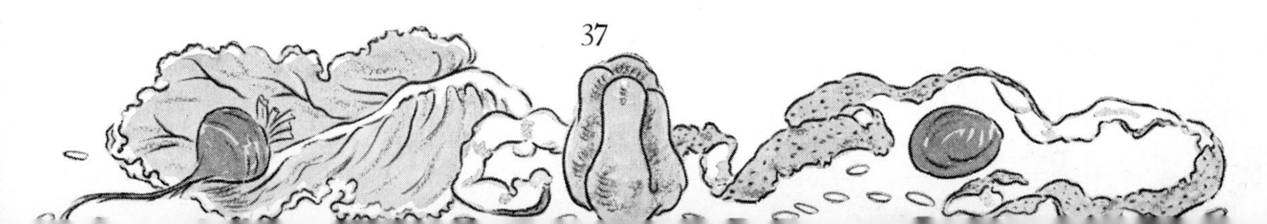

big speckled eggs. And they were very beautiful.

Marianka wished that Bidushka would lay the most beautiful egg in the world today, because tomorrow would be Easter and she wanted a surprise for her little sister, Nanka. So out from her pocket Marianka took the long red apple peeling. She gave it to Bidushka.

"Cluck-cluck!" said Bidushka, and ate it up.

Next Marianka gave Bidushka the lovely blue prune. Then she gave her the bright green pepper and the light green cabbage leaf. After that, Bidushka pecked at the purple beet. And finally Marianka sprinkled the white, white rice for her.

"Cluck-cluck!" said Bidushka, each time.

BIDUSHKA LAYS AN EASTER EGG

Marianka waited for Bidushka to lay an egg which would be speckled in red and blue and bright green and light green and purple and white. She waited all morning. But Bidushka did not lay that kind of egg. She did not lay any kind of egg.

Marianka waited all afternoon. She waited until nearly supper-time. Then she could wait no longer. She gathered up the little brown eggs and white eggs that the other hens had laid, and ran into the kitchen to Maminka.

"Maminka," said Marianka, giving her the six little eggs which she had gathered, "here are some eggs for you!"

"Good, good, good, my sweet raisin!" said Maminka. "Now I can stir up a lovely Easter cake!"

So Maminka tied on her apron, emptied the eggs into a bowl, and began to stir. While she was stirring, Marianka said, "Tt-tt-tt, Maminka!"

"Now what?" wondered Maminka.

"These are the things that Bidushka ate this morning!" said Marianka, counting on her fingers. "A long red apple peeling, a lovely blue prune, a bright green pepper, a light green cabbage leaf, a purple beet, and some white, white rice. You'd think Bidushka could have laid the most beautiful egg in the world by now, wouldn't you?"

"I certainly would!" laughed Maminka, stirring hard.

"It was going to be an Easter surprise for Nanka," said Marianka sadly.

"My sweet raisin," said Maminka, patting Marianka's cheek. "Na, run along! Tomorrow's time enough to see whether there is, or whether there isn't, a lovely surprise for Nanka."

So Marianka ran along.

Next morning the great green rooster crowed—

Rooka-roodle-oodle-oodle-oodle-oo!

Marianka jumped up to feed her chickens. She put on her clothes, tied her little red shawl over her head, and ran down the stairs to the kitchen.

There was Maminka, up already, baking her Easter cake, with the stove lit and her cheeks very pink.

"Maminka!" said Marianka, jumping up and down and clapping her hands.

She had never seen anything so lovely! Over the stove six little brown birds and white birds were flying. They were made out of empty eggshells, with heads of yellow paper and wings

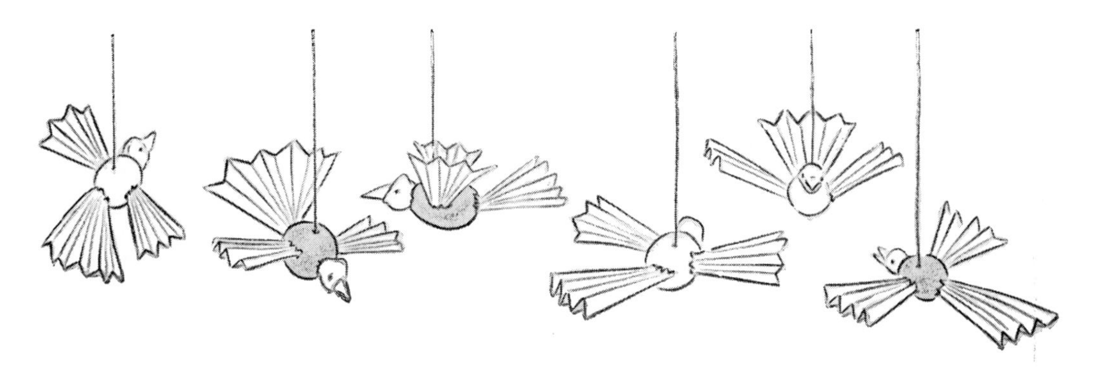

of yellow paper and long, long tails of yellow paper.

"Hsh!" whispered Maminka. "They are for Nanka!"

"Oh, Maminka!" whispered Marianka.

She was so happy that she filled the bowl to its very brim with chicken feed. She was so happy that she danced out past the barn to the place where the bare ground was.

"Come, chick-chick-chick! It's Easter!" said Marianka, very gaily, as she sprinkled chicken feed. "Come, chick-chick-chick!"

Her red hen, her white hen, and the great green rooster came. But not Bidushka. Where was she? Marianka ran to the chicken house. She flung open the door. And there she saw Bidushka, sitting on her nest.

"Bidushka!" said Marianka. "Have you laid an egg at last?"

"Cluckety-*awk!* Cluck! Cluck!" said Bidushka. And up she got.

"Oh! Oh!" cried Marianka. She had never been so surprised.

There in Bidushka's nest was a beautiful egg. It was not only speckled in red and blue and bright green and light green and purple and white! It was all covered, too, with little fancy stripes and flowers, as delicately done as lace! It was—*really!*—the most beautiful egg in the world.

"Oh, Bidushka!" said Marianka, giving her big speckled hen a hug. "Is it for me?"

"Cluckety-*awk!* Cluck! Cluck!" said Bidushka.

From *Maminka's Children*

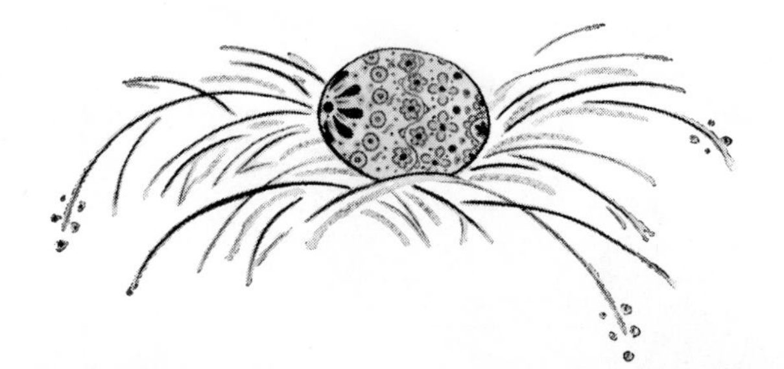

Dandi, the Deer

By Belle Coates

"WHAT kind of deer is he? Has he a name? Do tell me where you found him, and *why* you are painting his antlers *red?*"

The strange boy, Jerry Justice, had stopped at the Holland ranch in the Rockies to ask the way to the reservation, and he was all eyes and question marks about the pet deer.

"Dandi is a two-point, white-tailed buck," said Bill Holland, answering Jerry's first two questions as he began painting Dandi's left antler.

Jerry reached out and patted Dandi's back, and Bill could tell it was the first time Jerry had ever touched a live deer. Who could help patting gentle, brown-eyed, white-tailed Dandi?

"Two points on each antler means that Dandi is two years old," explained Bill's sister, Halfpint. "Next year there will be three points on each antler."

Halfpint was holding the can of red paint for Bill, and she blinked as if the turpentine in the paint smarted her eyes. But she went on answering Jerry's questions, for it was the rule at the Holland ranch to be hospitable. "I found Dandi under a berry bush over by the big pine the day I rode the wild deer and—"

"You rode a wild deer?" interrupted Jerry with a gasp. He

M·S·HURFORD

stared at this wispy, deer-riding Rocky Mountain girl as if she'd taken leave of her senses. He glanced toward her brother to see if he would smile at her little joke, but Bill painted soberly away as if riding wild deer was as common as peddling a bike.

"The day I rode the wild deer," Halfpint repeated calmly. "And we are painting Dandi's antlers red, so that when he goes out in the woods the hunters will know he is somebody's pet deer."

There was a catch in Halfpint's voice, and she wished that this strange boy would go. He had come running to them from the big black car yonder to ask the way through the mountains to the reservation. Now that they had told him, why didn't he go?

Truth to tell, Halfpint's heart was just about breaking. Bill's, too—though he was a boy and wouldn't let on. As soon as the antlers were painted, they would have to turn Dandi loose in the mountains with the hunters and coyotes and deep snows.

What if Dandi *was* born to the wild, as Dad had said, and knew a wild thing's way of taking care of himself? What if he *did* have red-painted antlers to warn off hunters, and slim, swift legs to flee coyotes? Oh, Dandi, Dandi!

You couldn't tell your troubles to strangers, although there was something about this eager, questioning boy that made Halfpint and Bill feel that he would do something about it if he could. But no one could do a thing about the forest fire that had roared down the mountain last August. It had eaten up their beautiful pine trees and lapped up their hay meadows and garden, leaving no crops to sell, no money to buy the winter groceries. The only thing they could do was to leave their home and Dandi and go live in Falls City, where Dad could get work in the lumber mills.

Jerry Justice, of course, didn't know about that. "So you rode a wild deer," he said. "I've heard tell that a deer sort of skims along above the ground, only letting down a foot now and then to give him a fresh start. It must be easy to hold on to a wild deer's back." He grinned, and Halfpint knew he thought she had been joking. "But I didn't ride on the wild deer's *back,*" she came back saucily. "I rode on his antlers."

"Ah me!" Jerry clapped his head with his hand and pretended to fall against the side of the barn. "Now I *know* you are joking."

"No, she isn't," said Bill, painting the tip of Dandi's left antler. "She really did; that's how she found Dandi."

"See there!" cried Halfpint.

"Tell me about it," begged Jerry.

Well, talking helped keep that lump down in her throat. "It happened when I was small," said Halfpint. "I was only eight, but I looked more like six. And Bill and I were weeding in the garden."

She pointed toward the garden below the barn. It had once been lush green, but was now as black as a tar carpet where the forest fire had swept it. Behind it, a grove of burned pine tree trunks stood black and bare, like giant sticks of licorice.

DANDI, THE DEER

"When we got tired of weeding," Halfpint continued, "we took our naps between the lettuce rows. A big, six-pointed wild deer came into our garden for lettuce and stopped and licked my face. I cried out and raised my arms, like this, and my sweater sleeve got caught on the big deer's antlers. That frightened the deer, and he made a dash for the woods. And I hung to his antlers by my sweater and bounced against his shoulder."

"I was scared," said Bill soberly. "I thought sure she'd be trampled. Or lost in the woods."

"And then?" gasped Jerry.

"And then the wild deer jumped over a log by the big pine and my sweater tore. You can see the place on the shoulder where Mother mended it. Then I fell off under a berry bush—almost on top of Dandi. I wasn't hurt."

"What was Dandi doing there?" demanded Jerry, who doubted no more.

"We never knew. He must have been lost from his mother almost as soon as he was born. Anyway, that's how we found him. He was so little that Dad carried him home under his coat. We fed him out of a bottle and taught him to come to our whistle."

Lovingly Halfpint stroked Dandi's side and his slim, curved neck. Dandi looked around at her out of his soft, trusting brown eyes. Then someone honked the horn in the big black car that crouched like a gentle dog in the road beyond the barn.

"Father's calling me," said Jerry, sidling toward the car. "Thanks for directing us to the reservation. My father is collector

for the museum in New York City, and we've come out west to collect Indian relics and beadwork. You don't happen to have any relics or beadwork to sell, do you?"

He paused and looked at them eagerly. These Rocky Mountaineers who rode wild deer and painted deer's antlers—no telling what they might have tucked away in their log cabin!

"No," said Halfpint, wishing that they *did* have something to sell, so they would have money to buy winter groceries and wouldn't have to leave their home, woods, and deer.

Jerry's father honked the car horn again and he had to go. "I hope I'll see you again sometime," he called back over his shoulder.

"We hope so, too," they said.

Jerry ran down the slope, stepped into the black car, and drove away.

Mother and Dad came out of the cabin, carrying the heavy old white buffalo robe between them. They stood in the dooryard and gave it a good shaking. Halfpint turned away.

The sight of the old white buffalo robe that had lain in mothballs all summer—indeed, for one hundred summers—reminded her that tomorrow morning the old robe would cover Bill's knees and hers against the frosty air. They would need it as they rode in the wagon down the mountain to Falls City.

Bill waved good-by to Jerry with his paintbrush. Then he

cleaned it on the side of the barn and laid it down. The antlers were painted. He had taken twice as long as he needed, and he had done a neat job.

"We'd better get going into the woods with Dandi. It's getting on in the day. Looks like snow over Bald Peak," he added, as if he didn't much care one way or the other.

Halfpint turned into the barn and took the jersey heifer's leather collar from the peg in the empty cow pen. The jersey heifer had been sold along with the pigs and chickens, because there was no feed for them. Dandi would wear the jersey heifer's leather collar and her tinkling brass bell into the woods. The tinkle of the brass bell would help the red-painted antlers warn off the hunters.

Bill buckled the jersey heifer's collar about Dandi's slim, curved neck and led him across the black-carpeted garden into the autumn woods. Halfpint walked with her hand on Dandi's back. Dandi, trusting one, did not dream that they must soon desert him. But the pheasant cock, who had lived in the meadow all summer, seemed to know. He stalked out of a rosebush thicket and stretched his white-ringed neck and scolded them roundly.

They passed the grove of burned pine trees and climbed beneath the great pines and firs and tamaracks that marched in stately columns up the side of the mountain.

There, beneath a spreading fir, Halfpint scratched the favorite

scratch-spot back of Dandi's ear, while Bill tore a great heap of tree moss from a low branch. Tree moss is to a deer what bread and strawberry jam are to us. Dandi didn't even look up for good-by as Halfpint and Bill left him munching the moss.

"There," muttered Bill, "that's over," meaning "Good-by." "That heap of moss will last Dandi for three days. He will never leave it until he's eaten the last crumb."

Halfpint blinked at a smarting in her eyes that no turpentine was to blame for. In three days, when Dandi came back to the cabin, he would find the door closed and the fireplace chimney empty of its curl of blue smoke. He would find no Bill or Halfpint, for they would be far away in a new school.

All that night Halfpint dreamed of tinkling brass bells; the woods seemed full of them. And Bill got lost in a forest of red antlers in his dream.

In the morning, when they rose at dawn at Mother's call in order to make an early start down the mountain, they found two surprises on their doorstep. Snow, from Bald Peak, deep and light as foam in the milk pail. And Dandi.

They stared at Dandi with his red antlers and tinkling bell and soft brown eyes. Dandi loved them better than all the tree moss in the Rockies. He had left his moss to come back to them. They hugged him and gave him heaping handfuls of rolled oats. "Oh, Dandi, to think that you have come back and still we must leave you behind," they thought.

What if Dandi wouldn't stay behind? "They don't let you keep a pet deer in an apartment house," said Halfpint. "You may perhaps have a puppy or a kitten, but not a two-point pet deer."

"After breakfast," decided Bill gruffly, "we'll take him over to the end of the lake. Dad saw a herd of white-tailed deer over there yesterday. Dandi will join the herd and forget about us."

They would have time. Since it had snowed in the night, Dad

must change the wagon box from the gear to the sled runners, then load the trunks.

"You're not eating your cereal," said Mother anxiously.

"We're not hungry."

"They're too excited about going on the trip," said Dad.

"We want to take Dandi over to the end of the lake to join the deer herd."

"Dandi will find the deer herd himself," said Dad kindly. "He's able to take care of himself."

But that wasn't it. They couldn't bear to coast merrily away in the sled and leave Dandi on the doorstep, staring mournfully after them with his ears turned toward them like brown sugar scoops. They couldn't bear to throw snowballs at him to drive him back if he followed.

So they took Dandi down the road that led to the reservation, then cut off through the woods at the end of the lake. They thought about Jerry and hoped he had reached the reservation before the snow came. They thought that the pines and firs and tamaracks marching toward the high white peaks were all very beautiful, coated with snow. Even the licorice sticks and tar carpet were beautiful now. It was almost as if there had never been a forest fire, except that, of course, there were still no groceries.

Dandi was the first to spy the herd of deer at the far end of the lake. Ting!—like that, he broke free of Bill's grasp and dashed toward his deer friends without so much as a backward glance.

Halfpint and Bill turned and started home. On the hill above the lake they looked around. Dandi was getting acquainted with the herd. He sniffed at their noses, and they sniffed at his painted antlers and at the strange scent of human hands upon his back. They drew away, then ran in circles through the snow around him.

"They'll probably make him their leader," said Bill. And he began to whistle, then stopped for fear he might whistle Dandi back to them. They told themselves they were quite happy at thinking how happy Dandi would be as the leader of the white-tailed deer.

When they reached home, Halfpint gathered straw for the bottom of the sled, while Bill hitched the team, and Dad loaded the trunks. Then Halfpint and Bill sat on the straw and Mother covered them with the old white buffalo robe, tucking it well about them. It was heavy and warm and yellowed with age. Great-grandfather Holland had got it from the Indians in 1836, and it was the only white buffalo skin known to be in the whole state of Montana at that time. There were thousands of brown buffaloes on the plains but only a very few white ones. The white ones were sacred to the Indians.

Then Mother was getting settled on the front seat. Dad picked up the reins. They were off. Halfpint and Bill closed their eyes against the sight of the receding log cabin with its locked door and empty fireplace chimney. They were thankful that Dandi was away, safe and happy with his deer friends.

Suddenly, as they whizzed out of the pasture gate, there came a rat-a-tat-tatting over the snow. A brown tinkling thing, with a flash of red before and a flicker of white behind, leaped out of nowhere into the bottom of the sled and stood at the feet of Halfpint and Bill.

It was Dandi! His eyes and his nostrils and his sugar-scoop ears were wide open and he was breathing hard.

"Wherever it is you are going, I want to go, too. I want to be with you, more than I want to be leader of all the white-tailed deer in the Rockies," he seemed to say.

Without a word, Halfpint and Bill reached out and took hold of Dandi as if they would never let go.

Mr. Holland halted the team. Very gravely he came to the back of the sled. There was a hushed silence, except for Dandi's breathing. What would Dad say? It would be like pulling their hearts out by the roots to leave Dandi now. There *must* be a place in Falls City for Dandi.

"Dad," began Bill, but that was as far as he got with his plea, for down the road came a loud, "Hi!"

And there was Jerry Justice hurrying through the snow with his father close behind.

"I found Dandi roaming about in the woods," Jerry panted, rushing up. "I think he had been playing with a herd of deer and was lost, so I whistled and caught him and brought him back. As soon as he saw you in the sled he broke away."

Halfpint and Bill, with their arms around Dandi, stared coldly at Jerry. Jerry thought he had done them a kind turn by bringing Dandi back. Jerry was a nice boy. But why didn't he go on and collect Indian relics and beadwork instead of meddling with their deer and breaking their hearts all over again?

"Jerry found your deer while we were walking back to see if you would haul our car out of a snowdrift with your team," Mr. Justice explained, then stopped short. "Why, there is a white buffalo robe!" Incredulously he fingered the old robe.

"White buffaloes were very rare," he said. "I should like to buy your white buffalo robe, Mr. Holland. I am a collector of relics for a museum in New York City. The museum will pay you—"

Mr. Justice named an amount of money—quite enough to buy winter groceries, to buy back the jersey heifer, the pigs, and the chickens. But Halfpint and Bill didn't pay much attention to the amount. They only knew that they were suddenly very rich. They had their beautiful white woods again, their strong log cabin. And they had their Dandi. They would not have to go to Falls City.

"Will you tell me how you came to have the white buffalo robe?" asked Jerry.

Halfpint and Bill wanted to be hospitable. They wanted to unlock their door and build a fire in the fireplace and tell Jerry how Great-grandfather Holland got the white buffalo robe. But for this first happy moment they could only smile at him from under the old robe and hug their dear Dandi.

Freddie the Great

By Ruth Cromer Weir

IT WAS six o'clock on a warm summer morning, and the newborn Guernsey calf lay quietly by his mother. Now and then he sniffed curiously at a new and beautiful world of green grass, blue sky, and fresh air.

His mother, standing beside him, tossed her head at the sound the other cows kept answering: "Co Boss! Co Boss!"

The calf raised his head and tried to scramble to his feet as Keith, eleven years old, came through the gate. The boy stopped short when he saw the calf, and a friendly grin spread over his face.

But as he came closer the mother lowered her head. Snorting, she charged toward Keith. The boy leaped quickly over the gate to get out of her way. Then he ran up the lane calling, "Uncle Carl! Come quick! I've found him! He's here! He looks like a little deer."

Soon the boy came back with his uncle. "He *is* a beauty," said Carl softly. "Another fine bull calf. I'm glad you called me. These mothers often get excited with their first calves."

Keith's uncle laid one hand on the cow's neck to quiet her. Then he reached down and picked up the calf. "Do you want to help carry him to the barn?"

Keith gently put his arms around the soft warm body and

RUDEEN

they all started up the lane.

"What shall we call him?" Carl asked.

The boy thought for a moment. "We have up to Ferdinand the Fifth already," he said finally. "Let's call this one Freddie."

Near the barn a man was waiting. His brows made a heavy black line shadowing his eyes. He looked at Freddie and licked his lips.

"H-m-m-m! Veal cutlets!" he said in a harsh voice. The calf roused with a start and kicked his slender legs.

Carl's jaw stiffened. But the man pretended not to notice. "How do I get to Route 61?" he added, heading for a car parked in the road.

"Straight north!" Carl's voice was sharp, and the new-born calf looked to see if it was the same gentle man who had picked him up. But Carl was smiling now. "Here we are," he said, as they put the calf on a bed of clean straw. "Whew, the next time you have to be carried we'll let the tractor do it!"

Keith stayed with Freddie for a few minutes, admiring the fawn-colored body and the long slender legs which ended in tiny divided hoofs. Freddie's shiny wet nose snubbed up at the end. His soft brown eyes were fringed in inch-long lashes. Keith stroked the silky ears.

"Now I must go to help Uncle Carl with your mother," he said. "Later you'll have to learn to drink from a pail. I'll be back," he added.

Freddie must have waited an hour, dozing in the pleasant

barn. The top of the barn was full of clover and alfalfa hay. It smelled good, mixed with the odor of warm milk. He wrinkled his nose and sniffed.

Then Keith dashed in with a bucket in his hand. "Here, Freddie," he said. The calf tried once more to stand, but he couldn't, and the boy sat down beside him. He tipped the bucket, just as though Freddie could take a drink from the edge. Then he put the calf's head in it and, in a moment, the calf was noisily sucking the warm milk. Keith grinned as he took the bucket away to let the calf rest. Freddie was panting, he had worked so hard to eat. The boy held the bucket to him again, and he drank almost all the milk.

"I'm going to take care of you from now on," Keith said. "You're my favorite because I found you myself."

Part of the barn lot had been fenced off for the calves where they were turned out to frisk and play as they grew older. There they could see the other farm animals and become used to cars, trucks, tractors, and other farm machinery.

By the time Freddie was two months old he spent most of each day in the lot. He bounded. He leaped. He kicked his hind legs into the air and looked surprised when he landed on all fours. But no matter how hard he was playing he could always hear Keith coming from a long way off and he was always waiting at the gate when he arrived.

When he got up from his straw bed in the morning, he stretched and s-t-r-e-t-c-h-e-d and every time he stretched he seemed to grow a little bigger. Then he ran out into the lot where he could hear Keith preparing the calves' breakfast in the granary—one shovel of calf meal, one shovel of whole oats, and two shovels of ground corn.

One morning after Freddie had eaten his breakfast and Carl and Keith were finishing their chores, a car swung into the drive and parked near the barnyard. A heavy-set man with a brown felt hat pulled low over his face walked to the fence.

Freddie ran to the fence and sniffed curiously, hoping to be petted. But when he came close he saw the heavy black brows under the man's hat brim. He put on his brakes and stopped short in his tracks. He rolled his big eyes round and round, showing the whites. Then he kicked his heels up in the air and whirled back into the lot, his tail standing straight out behind him.

The man paid no attention. He leaned on the top rail and looked past Freddie into the next lot where the steers were cleaning up their feeding of corn. "Twenty-eight, twenty-nine, thirty, thirty-one," the man counted under his breath. "Nice lot of steers, mister," he said when Carl crossed the lot and came up to him. "I'm a stock buyer. I'd like a collect a carload of steers. How about sending yours to market next month?"

"No, mine are all spoken for," Carl said shortly. Then he noticed Keith's white face. The boy had come up behind Carl in the lot. He stood with his arm around Freddie's neck. "I mean all except this one." Carl reached down and gently patted Freddie's head. "We're keeping him."

Carl waited for Keith's smile of relief, then he looked closely at the man. "Didn't you inquire the way to Route 61 earlier this summer?"

The man's face turned red. "No!" he said, "Never been around here before. Well, good-by. Sorry you aren't interested in marketing through me. I always get top prices."

Carl pushed his hat to the back of his head as he always did when he was worried. "Funny," he said, as he watched the man drive away. "I'm almost *sure* he's the same one who was headed north earlier this summer. I don't like the way he acts. There have been some mighty mysterious things happening in the next county. Tom Smithers lost ten head of his prize Herefords last week —worth over $3,000. Jack Cruthers lost twelve of his best hogs a while back." Carl looked thoughtfully into the distance at the car disappearing in a cloud of dust.

Freddie grew bigger and stronger every day. His head now reached Keith's shoulder. The inside of the barn seemed stuffy to him, and he began staying out in the lot all night. There he could hear the cattle stirring and the big bull, his father, restlessly pacing back and forth in his pen.

Beyond the windmill in an upper window of the neatly painted house Keith's head would appear every night and morning. He whistled or shouted a greeting to Freddie, and Freddie would answer with a loud cheerful "Baw."

One hot sultry night in late August, Freddie watched as Keith waved good night from his window. He played with the other calves for awhile, butting his head against them, pushing and shoving, pretending to lock horns in battle.

The lights went out in the house. The last locust buzzed its last buzz for the night. Even the crickets and katydids seemed to doze off, one by one. It was dark and quiet.

Freddie usually slept until the sun colored the eastern sky. But tonight he awakened with a start. He heard the noise of a motor coming up the lane. He staggered sleepily to his feet, his ears sticking straight out from his head. A big truck stopped almost in front of him and swung back against the fence. Two men jumped out and lowered boards over the fence to make a ramp for the cattle.

Freddie had never seen anything like this happen in the middle of the night. He stood watching and listening. Then one of the men flashed a light in Freddie's face.

"Psst," he whispered, "Look what's here. Didn't plan on taking this one, but beef is beef." He grabbed Freddie roughly and slipped a rope around his neck. "Now, my little friend, right this way," he said as he jerked the rope. The other man pushed from the rear. He twisted Freddie's tail. It hurt!

As the men pulled and pushed Freddie up the ramp, things started happening. Freddie was scared and he was *mad*. He pulled back with a snort and butted the man who was leading him. Turning, he swung at the man behind. He snorted and pawed and puffed. Then with a leap, he jerked his rope loose, jumped off the ramp, and ran to the center of the lot.

"Baw, baw, baw," he called. Suddenly a light shone from a window. "BAW!" called Freddie as loud as he could. His mother answered from the barn, "BAW—huh, BAW-huh!"

Then there was a roar and a bellow. It was Freddie's father. The farm buildings shook with the noise. Freddie stood bracing himself as the very ground seemed to tremble.

The whole barnyard came to life. The horses neighed. The pigs grunted and squealed. The roosters crowed. The hens cackled.

Meanwhile the lights had flashed on in all parts of the house. And now the farmyard lights blazed on.

FREDDIE THE GREAT

The men scrambled into the truck and zoomed down the lane as fast as they could travel.

Keith bounded out the back door in his blue-and-white striped pajamas. "Freddie, oh Freddie," he called as he tore down the walk to the barnyard. "Are you all right?"

Freddie jumped and ran toward the gate to meet him, but as he ran he tripped on the rope that still hung around his neck and nearly fell.

Keith's uncle was very quiet as he loosened the rope from the calf's neck. Then he went into the house to telephone.

Everyone was still making over Freddie a half hour later, when a car swung into the drive. "What's all the ruckus?" asked a man with a big silver star on his vest. It was the sheriff.

"Someone must have been after my steers," said Carl. "But this little fellow set off the alarm."

"Probably those men who've been hanging around pretending to be stock buyers," said the sheriff. "I've had my eye on them for several days."

Then he looked down at Keith who had his arm around the calf's neck. "This is Freddie, the calf that outwitted the robbers you're after," said Keith proudly. "From now on we're going to call him *Freddie the Great.*"

The Guernsey bull calf looked at the sheriff for a moment. Then he nuzzled against Keith's hand. He wanted to be petted.

A Miserable Merry Christmas

By Lincoln Steffens

WHAT interested me in our new neighborhood was not the school, nor the room I was to have in the house all to myself, but the stable which was built back of the house. My father let me direct the making of a stall, a little smaller than the other stalls, for my pony, and I prayed and hoped and my sister Lou believed that that meant that I would get the pony, perhaps for Christmas. I pointed out to her that there were three other stalls and no horses at all. This I said in order that she should answer it. She could not. My father, sounded, said that some day we might have horses and a cow; meanwhile a stable added to the value of a house. "Some day" is a pain to a boy who lives in and knows only "now." My good little sisters, to comfort me, remarked that Christmas was coming, but Christmas was always coming and grownups were always talking about it, asking you what you wanted and then giving you what they wanted

you to have. Though everybody knew what I wanted, I told them all again. My mother knew that I told God, too, every night. I wanted a pony, and to make sure that they understood, I declared that I wanted nothing else.

"Nothing but a pony?" my father asked.

"Nothing," I said.

"Not even a pair of high boots?"

That was hard. I did want boots, but I stuck to the pony. "No, not even boots."

"Nor candy? There ought to be something to fill your stocking with, and Santa Claus can't put a pony into a stocking."

That was true, and he couldn't lead a pony down the chimney either. But no. "All I want is a pony," I said. "If I can't have a pony, give me nothing, nothing."

Now I had been looking myself for the pony I wanted, going to sales stables, inquiring of horsemen, and I had seen several that would do. My father let me "try" them. I tried so many ponies that I was learning fast to sit a horse. I chose several, but my father always found some fault with them. I was in despair. When Christmas was at hand I had given up all hope of a pony, and on Christmas Eve I hung up my stocking along with my three sisters. I haven't mentioned them because, you understand, they were girls, and girls, young girls, counted for nothing in my manly life. They did not mind me either. They were so happy that Christmas Eve that I caught some of their merriment. I speculated on what I'd get; I hung up the biggest stocking I had, and we all went reluctantly to bed to wait till morning. Not to sleep; not right away. We were told that we must not only sleep promptly, we must not wake up till seven-thirty the next morning—or if we did, we must not go to the fireplace for our Christmas.

We did sleep that night, but we woke up at six A. M. We lay in our beds and debated through the open doors whether to obey till, say, half-past six. Then we bolted. I don't know who started it, but there was a rush. We all disobeyed; we raced to disobey and get first to the fireplace in the front room downstairs. And there they were, the gifts, all sorts of wonderful things, mixed-up piles of presents. But as I disentangled the mess, I saw that my stocking was empty. It hung limp; not a thing in it; and under and around it—nothing. My sisters had knelt down, each by her pile of gifts. They were squealing with delight, till they looked up and saw me standing there in my nightgown with nothing. They left their piles to come to me and looked with me at my empty place. Nothing. They felt my stocking: nothing.

I don't remember whether I cried at that moment, but my sisters did. They ran with me back to my bed, and there we all cried till I became indignant. That helped some. I got up, dressed, and driving my sisters away, I went alone out into the yard, down to the stable. And there, all by myself, I wept. My mother came out to me by and by. She found me in my pony stall, sobbing on the floor, and she tried to comfort me. But I heard my father outside; he had come part way with her. She besought me to come to breakfast. I could not; I wanted no comfort and no breakfast. She left me and went on into the house with sharp words for my father.

I don't know what kind of breakfast the family had. My sisters said it was "awful." They were ashamed to enjoy their own toys. They came to me, and I was rude. I ran away from them. I went around to the front of the house, sat down on the steps, and, the crying over, I ached. I was wronged, I was hurt—I can feel now what I felt then, and I am sure that if one could see the wounds upon our hearts, there would be found still upon mine a scar from that terrible Christmas morning. And my father, the practical joker, he must have been hurt, too, a little. I saw him looking out of the window. He was watching me or something for an hour or two, drawing back the curtain ever so little lest I catch him, but I saw his face, and I think I can see now the anxiety upon it, the worried impatience.

After—I don't know how long—surely an hour or two—I was brought to the climax of my agony by the sight of a man riding a pony down the street, a pony and a brand-new saddle. It was the most beautiful saddle I ever saw, and it was a boy's saddle. The man's feet were not in the stirrups; his legs were too long. The outfit was perfect; it was the answer to all my prayers. A fine new bridle, with a light curb bit. And the pony! As he drew near, I saw that the pony was really a small horse, what we called an Indian pony, a bay, with black mane and tail, and one white foot and a white star on his forehead. For such a horse as that I would have given, I could have forgiven, anything.

But the man, a disheveled fellow with a blackened eye and a fresh-cut face, came along, reading the numbers on the houses, and, as my hopes rose, he looked at our door and passed by, he and the pony, and the saddle and the bridle. Too much. I fell upon the steps, and having wept before, I broke now into such a flood of tears that I was a floating wreck when I heard a voice.

"Say, kid," it said, "do you know a boy named Lennie Steffens?"

I looked up. It was the man on the pony, back again, at our horse block.

"Yes," I spluttered through my tears. "That's me."

"Well," he said, "then this is your horse. I've been looking all over for you and your house. Why don't you put your number where it can be seen?"

"Get down," I said, running out to him.

He went on saying something about "ought to have got here at seven o'clock; he told me to bring the nag here and tie him to your post and leave him for you . . ."

"Get down," I said.

He got down, and he boosted me up to the saddle. He offered to fit the stirrups to me, but I didn't want him to. I wanted to ride.

"What's the matter with you?" he said, angrily. "What you crying for? Don't you like the horse? He's a dandy, this horse. I know him of old. He's fine at cattle; he'll drive 'em alone."

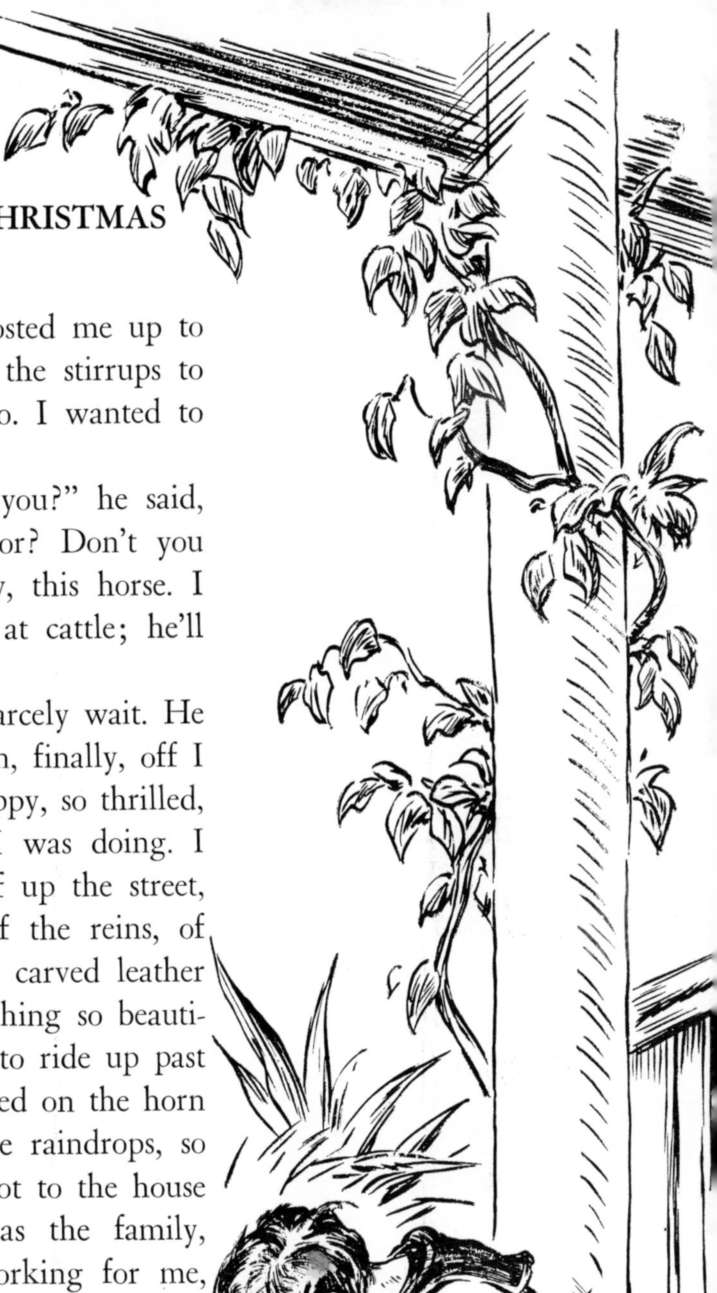

I hardly heard, I could scarcely wait. He adjusted the stirrups, and then, finally, off I rode, slowly, at a walk, so happy, so thrilled, that I did not know what I was doing. I did not look back. I rode off up the street, taking note of everything—of the reins, of the pony's long mane, of the carved leather saddle. I had never seen anything so beautiful. And mine! I was going to ride up past Miss Kay's house. But I noticed on the horn of the saddle some stains like raindrops, so I turned and trotted home, not to the house but to the stable. There was the family, father, mother, sisters, all working for me,

all happy. They had been putting in place the tools of my new business: blankets, currycomb, brush, pitchfork—everything, and there was hay in the loft.

"What did you come back so soon for?" somebody asked. "Why didn't you go on riding?"

I pointed to the stains. "I wasn't going to get my new saddle rained on," I said. And my father laughed. "It isn't raining," he said. "Those are not raindrops."

"They are tears," my mother gasped, and she gave my father a look which sent him off to the house. Worse still, my mother offered to wipe away the tears still running out of my eyes. I gave her such a look as she had given him, and she went off after my father, drying her own tears.

My sisters remained and we all unsaddled the pony, put on his halter, led him to his stall, tied and fed him. It began really to rain; so all the rest of that memorable day we curried and combed that pony. The girls plaited his mane, forelock, and tail, while I pitchforked hay to him and curried and brushed, curried and brushed. For a change we brought him out to drink. We led him up and down, blanketed like a race horse; we took turns at that. But the best fun was to clean him.

When we went to our midday Christmas dinner, we all smelt of horse, and my sisters had to wash their faces and hands. I was asked to, but I wouldn't, till my mother bade me look in the mirror. Then I washed up—quick. My face was caked with muddy lines of tears that had coursed over my cheeks to my mouth. Having washed away that shame, I ate my dinner, and as I ate I grew hungrier and hungrier. It was my first meal that day, and as I filled up on the turkey and the stuffing, the cranberries and the pies, the fruit and the nuts—as I swelled, I could laugh. My mother said I still choked and sobbed now and then, but I laughed, too. I saw and enjoyed my sisters' presents till—I had to go out and attend to my pony, who was there, really and truly there, the promise, the beginning, of a happy double life. And—I went and looked to make sure—there was the saddle, too, and the bridle.

But that Christmas, which my father had planned so carefully, was it the best or the worst I ever knew? He often asked me that; I never could answer as a boy. I think now that it was both. It covered the whole distance from broken-hearted misery to bursting happiness—too fast. A grownup could hardly have stood it.

From *Boy on Horseback*

A Little Black Bear Goes to School

By Evelyn Ray Sickels

"TAKE it back!" panted Henry, delivering a well-aimed blow at the struggling boy beneath him.

"Won't!" came the muffled but stubborn reply.

Then Sam, the boy underneath, gave a mighty lunge which sent both boys rolling over and over. Legs and fists flew. The fight was on again.

Neither of the boys saw the stranger who stepped into the clearing just in time to witness the fight. His clothes were tattered. His long gray hair fell almost to his shoulders. His blue eyes were bright with humor. But when he saw that the blows were smashing down in real earnest, he strode toward the boys.

"Hold on, you young wildcats!" he called. It was several moments before he succeeded in separating the clawing, struggling boys. Grasping each firmly by the collar, he said, "Now, then. Speak up. What's the trouble?"

"Sam says Johnny Appleseed is just an old tramp," cried

Henry, pushing the hair out of his eyes. "And I'm making him take it back."

The stranger's eyes twinkled. "Well, perhaps Johnny Appleseed *is* just an old tramp."

"Sure he is," muttered Sam.

"No, sir," cried Henry, ignoring Sam's remark. "You don't know him if you think that. He is kind to everybody. My pa says he walks hundreds of miles every year planting apple trees so the settlers can have fruit."

"What started you boys talking about Johnny Appleseed?" asked the stranger.

"He's going to teach school next week. The master is sick," said Sam. "And who wants to go to school to an old tramp?"

"He's not a tramp!" cried Henry.

"Well, now," drawled the stranger, "if old Appleseed is going to teach your school, why don't you wait? Judge him for yourselves! Then if you still want to fight, come back to this beech tree and have it out."

The boys eyed one another. Each was reluctant to be the first to give in. As the old man watched them, he took from his sagging pockets two red apples. He slipped one into the right hand of each boy just as that hand was closing into a fist. When the boys felt the firm, smooth fruit, they seemed to change their minds. Instead of fighting, they sank their teeth into the apples. They grinned at the stranger.

"Well, boys, I'll be going along," said the old man, stooping to pick up his bundle knotted to the end of a stick.

"Who are you, sir?" asked the boys.

"Oh, just a friend," he answered as he walked away.

That night it began to snow. By Monday morning the drifts were two feet deep. But all fifteen scholars managed to reach the little log schoolhouse. They were curious to see this man, Johnny

Appleseed, who had recently returned to Indiana from the Ohio country. They had heard so many stories about him. He seemed more like a legend than a real person.

As Sam and Henry approached the schoolhouse, each clung stubbornly to his own idea of Johnny Appleseed. Each boy was ready to fight to back up his opinion.

"Meet you at the old beech tree," muttered Sam, stamping off the snow.

"I'll be there first!" answered Henry, promptly.

Within the windowless schoolroom, the only light came from the blazing logs in the great fireplace. Whom should the boys see, sitting at the master's desk, but the old man who had interrupted their fight! His blue eyes flashed into a smile as he met their astonished gaze.

Johnny Appleseed was cutting open an apple to show the scholars the star hidden in the heart of the fruit. As Sam and Henry stumbled to their seats they heard him say, "I'll save these seeds. Come spring, I'll plant them near the schoolhouse. Maybe when your children and grandchildren come to this school, they will have apple trees of their own."

When it was time for school to begin, Johnny took an old, worn Testament from inside his coat. He turned the pages slowly.

"Look!" whispered Sam. "There's a hole right through the cover of the book!"

Johnny Appleseed smiled. "Yes, sonny, that hole was made by a bullet. An Indian took a shot at me when I was helping the wounded at the battle of Tippecanoe."

The scholars gave a gasp of astonishment.

"This Testament saved my life. The bullet stopped at the twelfth chapter of John. Suppose I begin to read there."

When he had finished, one of the boys said, "My pa says you have traveled way out West. Did you see any wild animals, Mr.

. . . Mr. . . . ?"

"My friends call me Johnny. I've only known you for about a quarter of an hour. But that's plenty long to become friends. Just call me Johnny."

"Yes, sir . . . Johnny, I mean. But . . . but *did* you see any wild animals?"

"Most every night I'd hear the scream of a panther, the cry of the wildcat. I recollect, one day I found a baby fawn caught in a tangle of vines and underbrush. It was crying piteously. When I had set it free, I picked it up and carried it in my arms. Presently, I saw the mother. She called for the fawn to come to her. I set the little fellow on his feet, but instead of scampering off, it followed me. Finally, I had to frighten him before he would run to his mother."

Sam had become so interested in Johnny's stories, he quite forgot that he had ever called him a tramp. Now he asked, wide-eyed, "Did you ever meet a bear?"

"Many a time. I'll never, as long as I live, forget one occasion.

It was in the dead of winter. The snow was as deep as it is right outside the schoolhouse. All day I had traveled through the woods. When night came, I looked for a cabin, but there was none in sight. I knew I'd have to camp out. I searched until I found a big, hollow log in which I could sleep. I built a fire and cooked some mush for my supper. Then I threw branches on the blaze and started to crawl into the log. But what was that strange noise? G-r-r-r! It was the growl of a wild animal! Yes siree! Old Mister Bear had thought that was a fine log too! That was where *he* was going to sleep! I backed out of that log quicker than I had gone into it, you can bet your buttons! 'A bed in the snow,' says Johnny Appleseed to himself, 'is better than a bed in a log—when there is a hungry bear in there, too!' That night I slept in the snow. Appleseed Johnny—he always respects the rights of bears!"

The children chuckled with delight. They failed to hear a

scratching at the schoolhouse door. Suddenly the door was pushed open. In walked a small black bear! The girls cried out. And as for the boys—their eyes nearly popped out of their heads! For a moment, the bear seemed as astonished as the children. He stopped and sniffed, swaying from side to side.

But Johnny was well acquainted with bears. "As I was saying," he continued calmly, "it's well to respect the rights of bears. I reckon this little fellow's hungry. Likely he came in hoping to find something to eat."

One of the little girls timidly pushed her lunch basket toward Johnny. He selected a thick piece of bread. He approached the bear slowly, talking to him gently.

Oh, how brave was Teacher! thought the little girls. The boys gazed at him with respect. The cub sniffed the bread. In no time at all, he had gobbled it up. When he had finished, he sat up on his haunches begging for more.

Now every lunch basket flew open! What a fine dinner the little black bear enjoyed!

"He must have been a pet at one time," mused Johnny. "I reckon he'd like to belong to some one again. At least until the winter is over."

The bolder of the boys jumped from their seats. How eager they were to be chosen! Johnny looked at them all. His eyes lighted upon Sam. Suddenly the boy remembered that he had called Johnny Appleseed a tramp. He turned as red as the firelight on the hearth. Slowly he sank into his seat again. But at the teacher's next words, his heart leaped for joy.

"Sam, do you reckon you and Henry could take care of this bear?"

"Oh, yes, sir!" cried Sam.

"Henry, can you and Sam look after this bear without getting into a fight?"

"We'll take good care of him, sir! We won't fight."

"All right, boys. I think you had better take him home now, and fix a place for him. After eating such a big dinner, he'll want to curl up and take a good long nap."

Rather cautiously Sam and Henry approached the bear. The cub, however, seemed to sense the fact that the boys were his new masters. He gave a little grunt and followed. His little sides stuck way out. Well they might! For weren't they stuffed with the dinnners of fifteen hungry children?

In the doorway the boys paused, whispering. Then they looked back at their new teacher.

"We have a name for the cub," said Sam.

"What are you going to call him?" asked the old man.

"We're going to call him 'Johnny,' sir, after you!"

From *The School Bell Rings*

Wappie's Surprise Cake

By Harriet Bunn

WAPPIE was a monkey from Africa, a Monga Bey, which is the same as saying that he was a very high-class monkey indeed. But Wappie wasn't conceited about it. He would have traded his fine title and his topknot willingly for some playmates. Wappie was lonesome. The week before Christmas he was so lonesome that if he'd known how he would have cried.

When he'd first come to the Northland, he had lived in a sunny garden with his own rock to sit on and trees to climb. He chattered to the birds and all the children played with him.

Now it was winter. Peggy went off to kindergarten, leaving her pet behind, and Peggy's mother moved him into the house. Outside white flakes fell from the gray sky and covered the grass, and the wind howled like a wild animal from the jungle.

Wappie cowered on his perch. He'd never seen snow before and he couldn't understand it. The children outside rolled the snow into balls and pelted each other, but nobody brought him any. Worse than that—his usually peaceful household was full of secrets. Peggy wrapped up packages and crackled red tissue paper instead of playing with him.

Usually when Wappie wanted to attract her attention he jiggled the latch of his cage. But now she seemed too busy to hear. Everybody bustled about that morning except Wappie. Moreover there was a queer smell in the air, a smell he knew, only he couldn't for the life of him think what it belonged to. It came and went as the door from the dining room to the kitchen swung open and shut again.

Wappie couldn't bear it. He felt he had to know why the jungle seemed so near. That smell made him hungry for pineapples and pawpaws and for breadfruit washed down with coconut milk.

"Coconut," squeaked Wappie in monkey talk. "Coconut," and the tall palms with their rustling leaves seemed to rustle close to his ear. Coconut! That was the yummy smell that had teased him from behind the kitchen door.

He must get out. He couldn't wait another minute. Such pictures it brought him! He could see his brothers rolling the hairy nuts along the ground and knocking them together. When they had cracked the nuts apart, they flung back their heads to drain the sweet milk.

A coconut was waiting for him in that kitchen. It must be! His sense of smell had never deceived him yet. His tongue licked around his lips as he thought about it. And now he must find a way to get some. His tense fingers clutched the latch and shook it. He would have that coconut or burst!

Suddenly that latch came off in his hand! Wappie was free. He peered out cautiously. Perhaps someone around the corner was waiting to laugh at him. He slammed his cage door to see if that would raise somebody. But it was the time in the afternoon when Cook took her nap and Peggy had gone to mail Christmas cards.

Wappie had the world to himself. Once again that delicious smell floated to his nostrils. He rubbed his stomach delightedly and sniffed. Then he followed the trail through the dining room to the door that led to the kitchen. Flattening himself upon the floor he put his nose to the crack under it. The coconut was behind that door! Hurling himself against it, he forced his way through with no more than a twinge of the tail.

He had expected to find a tall palm tree, with coconuts nestling under the leaves at the end of the strong rough trunk. For a moment his heart stopped beating. Could he, Wappie, who had smelled lions and snakes miles away, be mistaken about such a well-known smell as that? He climbed on a chair and sniffed again.

In the center of the kitchen table, round and white and smooth, stood the coconut cake that Cook had baked and frosted for Christmas! Wappie had traced the smell to its source.

Wappie leaped to the table and tried to put his arms around the cake, but it was too big for him. He had never imagined a coconut could be so big. Besides it was white and soft instead of hard and brown and hairy like coconuts he had known. It looked ready to eat. Probably Peggy was planning a present for him.

Wappie buried his face in the frosting. It was his secret, his package, his surprise. He remembered cushions he had seen in the chairs on the sun porch. Perhaps Cook had made it for him to sit on. He plumped himself down and felt the cake warm and soft beneath him. Now he possessed it all; his hands stroked its glittering sticky sides; his nails scraped off fistfuls and carried them to his mouth.

Oh bliss! Oh joy! It tasted even better than the raw coconut milk he had drunk from the shell. Perhaps the snow was coconut too. That it was for him he did not doubt.

The feast was well under way when Cook's footsteps sounded on the kitchen stairway and at almost the same moment Peggy came in the back door. There sat Wappie in the middle of the table, in the middle of the cake. He lifted white, frosty hands in welcome; his black eyes sparkled.

"Jg, chg, ker chee," he cried, sure that they would understand.

Cook screamed; her round pink face turned a horrid red. "Wappie," she cried in horror and pointed at the cake.

Peggy, his best friend, stood beside her, cold and unsmiling. Wappie looked from one to the other without knowing what to make of it. He rose slowly to his feet on top of the cake, still clinging to a chunk. His mouth, smeared with frosting, hung open in surprise. *What* had he done now?

"Wappie, get off that cake or I'll—" Cook's gesture was unmistakable.

Wappie lost his temper as fast as he did everything else. Each hair on his lean, little body stiffened, his topknot bristled, his chops stood out as though they had been made of wire. If she wanted the old cake she could have it, and right in the eye, too. Wappie stood up and aimed with the hunk in his fist. He spit the bite in his mouth onto the floor. He dug his long toes into the frosting and scuffed it out behind him like a chicken scratching sand.

Cook cast about for a tool of punishment; the broom presented itself. She raised it with a flourish and made for him. Wappie did not wait. What his mistake had been he did not know, but when lions stalked in the jungle one sought the tallest tree without delay. The kitchen chandelier was the nearest thing to it. Poised on the cake, he gathered up his tail and sprang into the air.

He grabbed the cord and hung on, sliding slowly down until he reached the bulb at the end. It came off and exploded with a loud pop. Wappie leaped for the top of the cupboard.

Crouched on the edge, he peeped down at the ruin below. His cushion of cake had cracked across; there were crumbs all over the floor, and a trail of frosting followed to the cupboard.

WAPPIE'S SURPRISE CAKE

"Wappie," screamed Cook, "come down at once!" The broom poked from behind. Wappie shuddered, more at her tone of voice than the prodding broomstick.

Plainly he could not stay there. Looking beyond Peggy's head he saw that the back door was still open. In their surprise they had forgotten to close it—it offered a way of escape! He could make it, if he could strike the swinging branch that grew such noisy fruit just right. (After all the branch was bare now; there was no more fruit to explode.) Once he had escaped from the jaws of a hungry tiger by a vine not unlike it. He reached the hanging electric cord just as the broom swept the top of the cupboard. One swing, two swings, three swings—beyond Peggy lay an endless white road of whatever it was that covered the ground.

Wappie swung madly up to the ceiling and out over their heads. Then he let go and dove for the door. He ran several steps through the snow before he realized that he'd made another mistake. This strange something under his feet didn't feel right. He leaned down and took a bite. Why, it wasn't coconut flakes

FIORE MASTRI

that had dropped from the sky at all! It was a new icy stuff, colder than anything he had ever felt. Shivers slid from his teeth to his spine and down to the tips of his long, black toes. Even his tail felt chilled.

He ran on a few steps, but now his feet ached as though he had trod on a thorn bush. Each new step was agony. The bottom had dropped out of Wappie's world!

Just ahead rose the grandfather elm whose leafy depths he had explored during the warm weather. It looked bare enough now. But Wappie had to get his feet off the ground. He scrambled for a low branch and huddled there, a moist muff of black fur with chattering teeth.

And there Peggy found him a few minutes later, gazing down at her with sad dark eyes.

"Come down, Wappie darling," she coaxed.

Wappie only scrunched himself closer together on his perch and shook his head.

Suddenly Peggy remembered bananas. Wappie adored bananas. She ran to the kitchen and back again. "Very good banana, Wappie!"

A breath of banana reached Wappie from where he clung. There was certainly nothing fake about that. And Peggy was smiling.

WAPPIE'S SURPRISE CAKE

Wappie reached out a little black claw. As he grabbed the banana, Peggy caught him by the back of the neck and tucked him inside her fur-lined coat, banana and all. The warmth of the coat soothed him. Wappie snuggled close to Peggy's neck and laid a tired head against her shoulder.

That afternoon a happy monkey, bathed and brushed and dressed in his red plush jacket, sailed into the dimly lighted living room on Peggy's shoulder.

In one corner stood a tall green tree, its branches laden with tinsel and packages and bright lights. Never in Wappie's life had he seen a tree like that. He shook with excitement. Lots of things on that tree must be good to eat. His little eyes blinked as he peered at one ornament after another.

Peggy patted his red jacket. "Better stay here, Wappie. I'll find your present."

From a heap of packages at the bottom of the tree she selected one and laid it in his claws. "For you, Wappie. Merry Christmas!"

Wappie tore it open like a whirlwind. Inside a gay tin box lay what remained of the coconut cake. While the rest of the family admired their presents, Wappie ate cake. But he had one eye on the Christmas tree all the time. The fruit on that tree beat everything in the jungle. And on the topmost branch glittered a beautiful star.

"A star," gurgled Wappie in his best monkey talk, "a star for me!" He had tried to reach stars through the green palms of the jungle, but they were always too high for him.

Tonight he was satisfied. His stomach was full of cake, but the very next chance he got he was going to taste that star.

"Dear little Wappie," thought Peggy. "How he loves the tree! Tomorrow I must bring him in to see it again."

"Tomorrow," thought Wappie. "While they take their naps, I'll wriggle through the door and climb up and taste that star!"

*The Spoonbill and the Cloud**

By W. H. Hudson

As MARTIN grew in years and strength, his age being now about seven, his rambles began to extend beyond the waste grounds outside the fenced orchard and gate. Every day he ran down to the stream to gather flowers and shells, for many curious water snails were found there with brown purple-striped shells. And he also liked to watch the small birds that built their nests in the rushes.

*From *A Little Boy Lost* by W. H. Hudson, by permission of Alfred A. Knopf, Inc., copyright 1920 by Alfred A. Knopf, Inc.

There were three of these small birds that did not appear to know that Martin loved them; for no sooner would he present himself at the stream than forth they would flutter in a great state of mind. One, the prettiest, was a tiny, green-backed little creature, with a crimson crest and a velvet-black band across a bright yellow breast. This one had a soft, low, complaining voice, clear as a silver bell. The second was a brisk little gray and black fellow, with a loud, indignant "chuck," and a broad tail which he incessantly opened and shut, like a Spanish lady playing with her fan. The third was a shy, mysterious little brown bird, peering out of the clustering leaves, and making a sound like the soft ticking of a clock. They were like three little men, an Italian, a Dutchman, and a Hindoo, talking together, each in his own language, and yet well able to understand each other. Martin could not make out what they said, but suspected that they were talking about him.

At length he made the discovery that

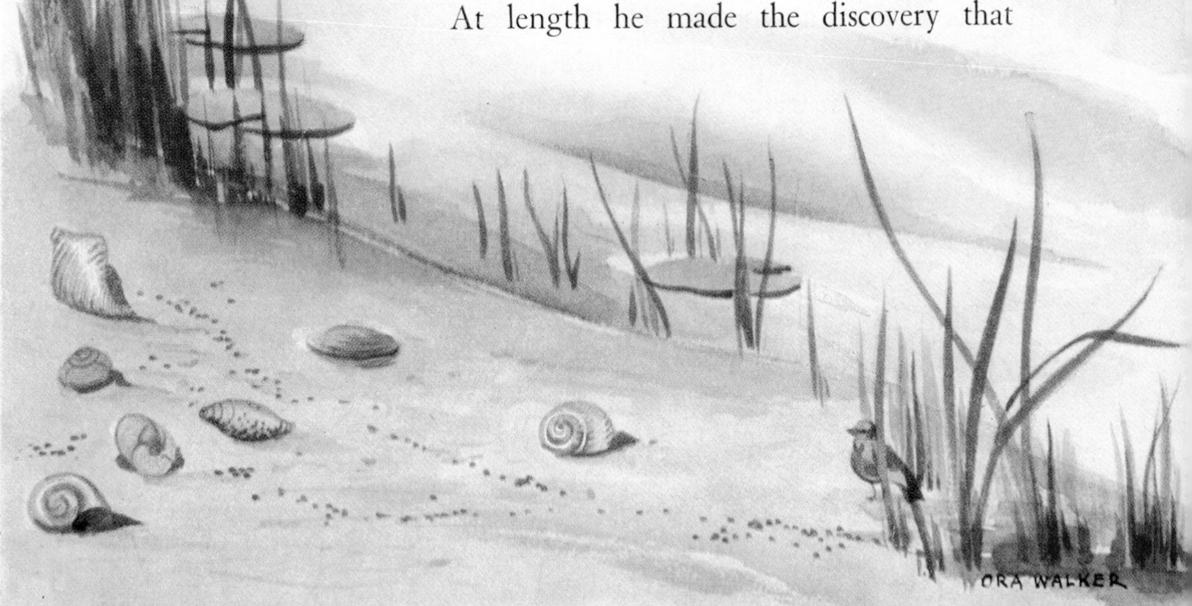

ORA WALKER

the water of the stream was perpetually running away. Whither did this rippling, running water go? He was anxious to find out. At length, losing all fear and fired with the sight of many new and pretty things he found while following it, he ran along the banks until, miles from home, he came to a great lake he could hardly see across, it was so broad. It was a wonderful place, full of birds; not small, fretful creatures flitting in and out of the rushes, but great majestic birds that took very little notice of him. Far out on the blue surface of the water floated numbers of wild fowl, and chief among them for grace and beauty was a swan, pure white with black head and neck and crimson bill. There also were stately flamingoes, stalking along knee-deep in the water, which was shallow. Nearer to the shore were flocks of rose-colored spoonbills and solitary big gray herons standing motionless; also groups of white egrets, and a great multitude of glossy ibises, with dark green and purple plumage and long sicklelike beaks.

The sight of this water with its beds of rushes and tall flowering reeds, and its great company of birds, filled Martin with delight; and other joys were soon to follow. Throwing off his shoes, he dashed with a shout into the water, frightening a number of ibises. Up they flew, each bird uttering a cry repeated many times, that sounded just like his old father's laugh, when he laughed loud and heartily. Then what was Martin's amazement to hear his own shout and this chorus of bird "ha, ha, ha's," repeated by hundreds of voices all over the lake. At first he thought that the other birds were mocking the ibises; but presently he shouted again, and again his shouts were repeated by dozens of voices. This delighted him so much that he spent the whole day shouting himself hoarse at the waterside.

When he related his wonderful experience at home, and heard from his father that the sounds he had heard were only echoes from the beds of rushes, he was not a bit wiser than before. The echoes remained to him a continual wonder and source of never-failing pleasure.

Every day he would take some noisy instrument to the lake to startle the echoes. A whistle his father made him served for a time. After that he marched up and down the banks, rattling a tin canister with pebbles in it. Then he got a large frying-pan from the kitchen, and beat on it with a stick every day for about a fortnight. When he grew tired of all these sounds, and began casting about for some new things to wake the echoes with, he all at once remembered his father's gun—just what he wanted, for it was the noisiest thing in the world. Watching his opportunity, he succeeded in carrying it out of the house without being seen. Then, full of joyful anticipations, he ran as fast as the heavy gun would let him to his favorite haunt.

When he arrived at the lake three or four spoonbills—those beautiful, tall, rose-colored birds—were standing on the bank, quietly dozing in the hot sunshine. They did not fly away at his approach, for the birds were now so accustomed to Martin and his harmless noises that they took little notice of him. He knelt on one knee and pointed the gun at them.

"Now, birdies, you don't know what a fright I'm going to give you—off you go!" he cried, and pulled the trigger.

The roar of the loud report traveled all over the wide lake, creating a great commotion among the feathered people, and they rose up with a general scream into the air.

All this was of no benefit to Martin, the

recoil of the gun having sent him flying over, his heels in the air. Before he recovered himself the echoes were silent, and all the frightened birds were settling on the water again. But there, just before him, lay one of the spoonbills, beating its great rose-colored wings against the ground.

Martin ran to it, full of keen distress, but was powerless to help. Its life's blood was fast running away from the shot wounds it had received in its side, staining the grass with crimson. Presently it closed its beautiful ruby-colored eyes and the quivering wings grew still.

Then Martin sat down on the grass and began to cry. Oh,

that great bird, half as tall as himself, and so many times more lovely and strong and beautiful in its life—he had killed it, and it would never fly again! He raised it up tenderly in his arms and kissed its pale green head and rosy wings; then out of his arms it tumbled back again on to the grass.

"Oh, poor bird," he cried suddenly, "open your wings and fly away!" But it was dead.

Then Martin got up and stared all round him at the wide landscape, and everything looked strange and dim and sorrowful. A shadow passed over the lake, and a murmur came up out of the rushes that was like a voice saying something that he could not understand. A great cry of pain rose from his heart and died to a whisper on his lips; he was awed into silence. Sinking down upon the grass again, he hid his face against the rosy-breasted bird and began to sob. How warm the dead bird felt against his cheek—oh, so warm—and it could not live and fly about with the others.

At length he sat up and knew the reason of that change that had come over the earth. A dark cloud had sprung up in the southwest, far off as yet, and near the horizon; but its fringe already touched and obscured the low-hanging sun, and a shadow flew far and vast before it. Over the lake flew that great shadow: the waters looked cold and still, reflecting as in a polished glass the motionless rushes, the grassy bank, and Martin, sitting on it, still clasping in his arms the dead, rose-colored bird.

Swifter and vaster, following close upon the flying shadow, came the mighty cloud, changing from black to slaty gray. Then, as the sun broke forth again under its lower edge, it was all flushed with a brilliant rose color. But what a marvelous thing it was, when the cloud covered a third of the wide heavens, almost touching the horizon on either side with its winglike extremities. Martin, gazing steadily at it, saw that in its form it was like an immense spoonbill flying through the air! He would gladly have run away then to hide himself from its sight, but he dared not stir, for it was now directly above him. So, lying down on the grass and hiding his face against the dead bird, he waited in fear and trembling.

He heard the rushing sound of the mighty wings. The wind they created smote on the waters in a hurricane, so that the reeds were beaten flat, and a great cry of terror went up from all the wild birds. It passed, and when Martin raised his bowed head and looked again, the sun, just about to touch the horizon with its great red globe, shone out, shedding a rich radiance over the earth and water; while far off, on the opposite side of the heavens, the great cloud-bird was rapidly fading out of sight.

After what had happened Martin could never visit the water-side and look at the great birds wading and swimming there without a feeling that was like a sudden coldness in the blood of his veins. The rosy spoonbill he had killed and cried over, and the great bird-cloud that had frightened him, were never forgotten. He grew tired of shouting to the echoes. He discovered that there were even more wonderful things than the marsh echoes in the world, and that the world was bigger than he had thought it.

From *A Little Boy Lost*

A Bird Cage with Tassels

By Anne Parrish

A LITTLE brown bird the color of a dead leaf had been hopping about on the ground under the chrysanthemums looking for something for its supper, and now suddenly flew up into a willow tree and began to sing.

The Little Emperor clapped his hands, and all his servants dropped on their knees and began to kowtow.

"Catch me that little brown bird with the beautiful song!" he said. He stopped yawning, and his eyes grew bright.

"But, Little Old Ancestor, that is such a plain little bird," said his aunt timidly. "Surely you would rather have a cockatoo as pink as a cloud at dawn, or a pair of lovebirds as green as leaves in spring—"

The rude Little Emperor paid not the slightest attention to her, but stamped his foot and shouted:

"Catch me that little brown bird!"

So his servants chased the poor little fluttering bird with butterfly nets. The wind whipped their bright silk skirts, and their pigtails streamed out behind, and they puffed and panted, for they were most of them very fat.

At last the bird was caught, and put in a cage trimmed with tassels of purple silk and pearls, with drinking cup and seed cup made like the halves of plums from purple amethysts on brown amber twigs with green jade leaves.

For a time the Little Emperor was delighted with his new pet, and every day he carried it in its cage when he went for a walk. But it never sang, only beat against the bars of its cage, or huddled on its perch. So presently he grew tired of it, and it was hung up in its cage in a dark corner of one of the Palace rooms, where he soon forgot all about it.

How could the little bird sing? It was sick for the wide blue roads of the air; for wet green rice fields where the coolies stand with bare legs, sky-blue shirts, and bamboo hats as big as umbrellas; for the yellow rivers, and the mountains bright with red lilies.

How could it sing in a cage? But sometimes it tried to cry to them: "Let me out! Please, *please* let me out! I have never done anything to harm you! I am so unhappy I think my heart is breaking! *Please* let me go free!"

"What a sweet song!" everybody would say. "Run and tell the Little Emperor that his bird

HANDFORTH

is singing again."

After a while the little bird realized that they did not understand, and it tried no longer, but drooped, dull-eyed and silent, in its cage.

One night the Little Emperor had a dream. Perhaps you won't wonder when I tell you what he had for supper.

First he had tea in a bowl of jade as round and white as the moon, heaped up with honeysuckle flowers.

Then, in yellow lacquer boxes, sugared seeds, sunflower and lotus flower and watermelon seeds, boiled walnuts, and lotus buds.

Then velvety golden peaches and purple plums with a bloom of silver on them.

Pork cooked in eleven different ways: chopped, cold, with red beans and with white beans, with bamboo shoots, with onions, and with cherries, with eggs, with mushrooms, with cabbage, and with turnips.

Ducks and chickens stuffed with pine needles and roasted.

Smoked fish.

Shrimps and crabs, fried together.

Shark fins.

Boiled birds' nests.

Porridge of tiny yellow seeds like birdseed.

Cakes in the shape of seashells, fish, dragons, butterflies, and flowers.

Chrysanthemum soup, steaming in a yellow bowl with a

green dragon twisting around it.

When he was so full that he couldn't hold anything more, not even one sugared watermelon seed, they took off his silk napkin embroidered with little brown monkeys eating pink and orange persimmons. He was so sleepy that he did not even stamp his feet when they washed his face and hands. Then they took off his red silk gown embroidered with gold dragons and blue clouds and lined with soft gray fur, his yellow silk shirt, and his red satin shoes with their thick white soles. But he went to bed in his pale yellow pantaloons, tied around the ankles with rose-colored ribbons.

I must tell you about his bed. It was made of brick, and inside of it a small fire was built to keep the Little Emperor warm. On top of this three yellow silk mattresses were placed, then silk sheets, red, yellow, green, blue, and violet, then a coverlet of yellow satin embroidered with stars. Under his head were pillows stuffed with tea leaves; and above him was a canopy of yellow silk, embroidered with a great round moon whose golden rays streamed down the yellow silk curtains drawn around him.

He fell asleep, and this is what he dreamed.

The long golden rays seemed to turn into the bars of a cage. Yes, he was in a huge cage! He tried frantically to get out! He beat against the bars! Then he saw what looked like the roots of

trees,
and brown
tree trunks, a
grove all around the
cage. But the trees moved
and stepped about. Looking up
the trunks, instead of leaves he saw
feathers, and still farther, sharp beaks, and
then bright eyes looking at him. They were birds!

What he had thought were the roots of trees were their claws, and the trunks of the trees were their legs. But what enormous birds! They were as big as men, while he was as small as a bird.

"Let me out!" he shouted. "Don't you know I am the Emperor, and every one must obey me? Let me out, I say!"

"Ah, he is beginning to sing," said one bird to another.

"Not a very musical song. Too shrill by far! Take my advice, wring his neck and roast him."

"Oh, let me out! Please, *please* let me out!" cried the poor Little Emperor in terror.

"He is singing more sweetly now," remarked one of the birds.

"Too loud! Quite ear-splitting!" said a lady bird, fluffing out her breast feathers and lifting her wings to show how sensitive she was.

A BIRD CAGE WITH TASSELS

"If he were mine, I should pluck him. His little yellow silk trousers would line my nest so softly."

"Oh, please, *please* set me free!"

"Really, his song is growing quite charming! But one can't stand listening to it all day."

And with a great whir and flap and rustle of wings, the birds flew away and left him in his cage, alone.

He called for help and threw himself against the bars until he was exhausted. Finally, growing hungry and thirsty, he looked

in his seed and water cups, drank a little lukewarm water, and ate a dry bread crumb. Now and then birds came and looked at him. Some of them tried to catch his pigtail with their beaks or claws.

Next day the Little Emperor was thoughtful. Could it be, he wondered, that a bird's nest was as dear to it as his own bed with its rainbow coverlets and its moon and stars was to him? That a bird liked ripe berries and cold brook water as much as he liked ripe peaches and tea with jasmine flowers? That a bird was as frightened when he tried to catch its tail in his fingers as he was when the birds tried to catch his pigtail?

Then he thought of how he had felt when the lady bird had wanted his pantaloons to line her nest. Hot with shame, he remembered his glistening jewel-bright blue cloak made of thousands of kingfishers' feathers. It had made him miserable to think of their taking his clothes, but suppose his clothes grew on him as their feathers did on them? How would he have felt then, hearing the birds say: "*I* should pluck him. His silk trousers would line my nest so softly"?

He went to bed thinking about his little brown bird, and he made up his mind to set it free in the morning.

Then he fell asleep, and once again he dreamed that he was in the golden cage.

Whir-rr! One of the great birds flew down by the cage door. With his claw he unfastened it—opened it!

Oh, how exciting! The Little Emperor tore out, so afraid he would be stopped and put back in the cage!

Oh, how he ran across the room and through the open door! Free! He was free! Tears rushed to his eyes, and his heart felt as if it would burst with happiness.

But it was winter. The garden was deep in snow that was falling as if it would never stop. The peaches and plums were gone, and the lotus pond was frozen hard as stone.

A BIRD CAGE WITH TASSELS

The Little Emperor had never been out in the snow before except when he was dressed in his warm padded clothes, with one Gentleman-in-Waiting carrying his porcelain stove, and another bringing tea, and a third with cakes in a box of yellow lacquer, and a fourth holding between the snowflakes and the Imperial head a great, moss-green umbrella. So small and helpless in so big and cold a world, what could a boy find to eat or drink? Where could he warm himself? He ran through the snow. The rose-colored ribbons that tied his pantaloons came untied and trailed behind him, and the cold snow went up his bare legs.

Pausing to catch his sobbing breath, he looked up to see the thick snow sliding from a pine tree branch, and jumped aside just in time to keep from being buried beneath it. Then on he plunged again, growing with each step more weak and cold and hungry; stopping now and then to call for help in a quavering voice that grew feebler every time; blinking back the tears that froze on his lashes as he tried to remember that emperors must never cry.

Then, as it began to grow dark, he saw two great lanterns shining through the snow, coming slowly nearer. Perhaps his aunt and his Chief Gentleman-in-Waiting, Lord Mighty Swishing Dragon's Tail (Lord Dragon Tail, for short) had missed him and had come with lanterns to look for him! He tried to go toward them, to call, but he was too exhausted to move or make a sound.

And then, imagine his terror when he realized that the glowing green lights were not lanterns at all, but the eyes of a great crouching animal—a cat!

Gathering all his strength for one last desperate effort, he tried to run. But with a leap the cat was after him, and with a paw now rolled into a velvet ball, now unsheathing sharp curved claws, tapped him first on one side, then on the other, nearly let him go, caught him again with one bound, and with a harder blow sent him spinning into stars and darkness.

Some one was shaking him. Was it the cat? The Little Emperor opened his eyes and saw the frightened face of Princess Autumn Cloud bending over him, as yellow as a lemon, for she had jumped up out of bed when she heard him cry out, and there hadn't been time to put on the honey and the powder, to paint on the surprised

black eyebrows or the round red mouth.

"Wake up, wake up, Little Old Ancestor!" she was crying as she shook him. "You're having a bad dream!"

"Aren't you the cat?" asked the Little Emperor, who wasn't really awake yet.

"Certainly *not,* Little Old Ancestor!" replied his aunt, rather offended.

The Little Emperor climbed out of his bed. The room was full of the still white light that comes from snow. Looking out of the window he saw that the plum trees and the cherry trees looked as if they had blossomed in the night, the snow lay so white and light on every twig. Softly the snow fell; deep, deep it lay; and the people who passed by his windows went as silently as though they were shod in white velvet.

The Little Emperor thought of his dream, and decided that his little bird might suffer and die if he let it go free before winter was over. But he explained to the bird.

"When summer comes, you shall fly away into the sky," he told it. He brought it fruit and green leaves to peck at, talking to it gently. And the little bird seemed to understand. The dull eyes grew brighter; and though it never sang it sometimes chirped as if it were trying to say, "Thank you."

On the first night of summer when the moon lay like a great round pearl in the deep blue sea of the sky, the Little Emperor slept, and dreamed again that the cage door opened for him and let him go free. But oh, what happiness now, happiness almost too great for a little boy to bear.

Peonies were in bloom, each petal like a big seashell, and blue butterflies floated over them in the warm sunshine. Half hidden in the grass the Little Emperor found a great purple fruit—a

TH

mulberry. How good it was!

The dewy spiderwebs glistened like the great tinsel Bridge to Heaven they built for him on every birthday. How happy he was! With the sun to warm him and the breeze to cool him; with food tumbling down from Heaven or the mulberry trees, he wasn't sure which, with a crystal clear dewdrop to drink on every blade of grass. How happy he was!

The lake was full of great rustling leaves and big pink lotus flowers. Venturing out on one of the leaves, he paddled his feet over its edge in the gently lapping water. Then, climbing into one of the pink blossons, he lay, so happy, so happy, looking up at the blue-green dragonflies darting overhead, and rocking gently in his rosy boat.

No, it was not the lotus flower that rocked him on the water. It was Princess Autumn Cloud who was gently shaking him, and saying, "Wake up, if you please, dear Little Old Ancestor!" And hard as it is to believe, she was really smiling. The Little Emperor had been so good lately.

He could not wait until after breakfast to let his brown bird go free. As soon as he was dressed, he ran as fast as he could to the room where the bird cage hung. Pat-a-pat-pat went his feet in their blue satin shoes, and thud, thud! puff, puff! his fat old Gentlemen-in-Waiting lumbered along behind him.

"I've come to set you free!" he whispered, as he carried the cage with its tassels of purple and pearls out into the beautiful day. For one minute he wanted to cry, for he had grown to love the little bird. But he remembered again that emperors must not

cry. He opened the door of the cage.

"Little Old Ancestor's bird has flown away!" cried the Mandarins.

"It has flown so high in the sky that we can hardly see it," the Court Ladies answered. And they all wished that the Little Emperor would stop gazing up into the sky at the little dark speck, so that they might go in and have their breakfasts.

But the Little Emperor, the empty bird cage in his hand, still looked up. High, high in the sky! And now, really, he could no longer see it. But a thread of song dropped down to him, a silver thread of song, a golden thread of love between the hearts of a little bird and a little boy.

From *The Dream Coach*

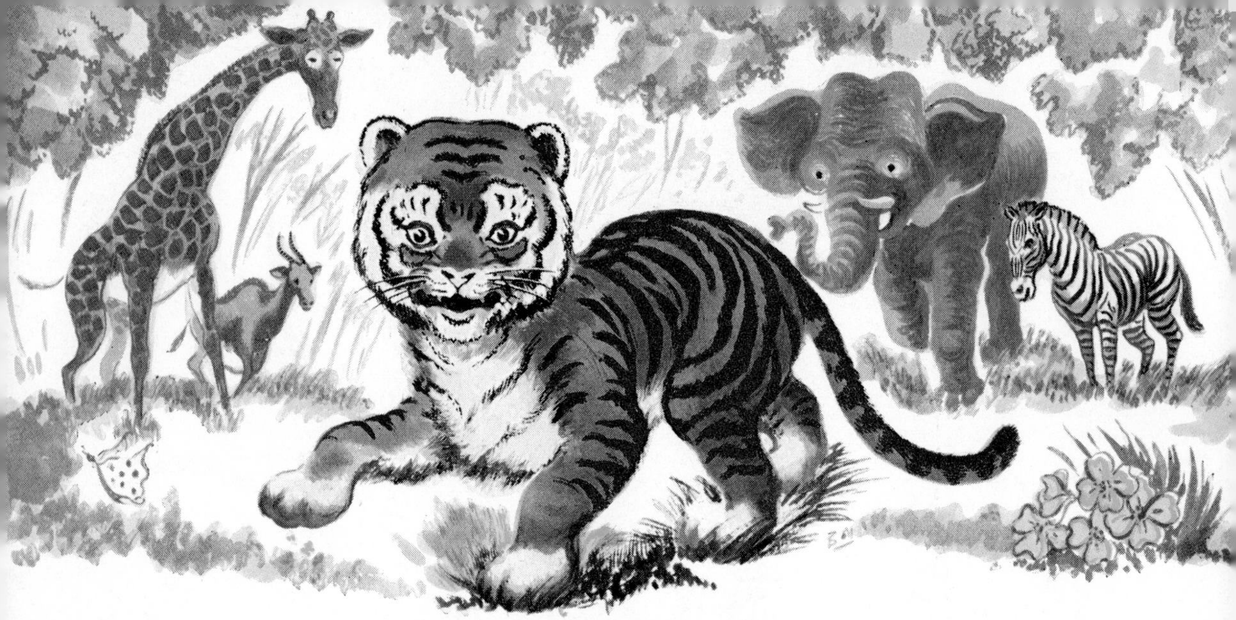

*The Story of Kattor**

By Georgia Travers

KATTOR was a baby tiger. He had a beautiful coat of yellow striped with black. His paws were as big as the boughs of a young tree and his tail was fine and swishy. His eyes were yellow and fierce, even for a small tiger's. He had a pink rough tongue which showed behind strong white teeth whenever he growled.

Kattor lived with his mother in a den of rocks in a hillside. Here he had a bed of dry crackly leaves. When he was very young he liked to lie there all day and to amuse himself by stretching out his big paws and by putting out the great claws which were hidden in the soft furry pads of his feet.

As he grew older his mother began taking Kattor out for exercise. Then he would jump about, turn somersaults, toss sticks into the air, and tear leaves to pieces with his sharp claws. He would strike playful blows at things with his front paws. He would pounce in fun at stones and shadows.

So Kattor lived and grew. Each day as he played out of doors he seemed to feel himself getting stronger and stronger.

Many months went by. Then one day Kattor ventured out all

* Reprinted by permission of Coward-McCann, Inc., copyright 1939 by Flavia Gág and Georgia Travers.

alone. He sharpened his claws on a great tall tree. He struck playfully at objects in his path. It was fun to crush them at a single blow. Wherever he went, all the other little creatures of the woods ran away screaming for their lives. This was very thrilling. How big and powerful he was!

That evening he went home and told his mother all he had done.

"I am a great strong tiger, am I not?" said Kattor.

"You are a strong *baby* tiger," said his mother. "But now you must sleep," and she fluffed up his bed of leaves, washed him tenderly with her great rough tongue, and purred to him softly as he went to sleep.

Every day after that Kattor went a little farther from home. Every day he sharpened his claws—and every day he dared to frighten bigger and bigger animals. And every night he would return to his mother and say as before, "Mother, I am a great strong tiger, am I not?" And every night his mother would reply, "You are a strong *baby* tiger." Then she would wash him with her great, rough tongue, fluff up his bed of leaves, and purr softly to him until he went to sleep.

This went on for a long time. Then one day as he was sharpening his claws on a tree, he ripped and scratched so fiercely into the bark that he felt even stronger than he had ever felt before. That day he went to hunt for food for the first time and brought it home proudly to show his mother.

"Mother, I am a great strong tiger, am I not?" said Kattor. And that night his mother answered, "Yes, Kattor, you are getting to be a great strong tiger."

"Some day I will conquer the world for you," said Kattor.

"Do well what tigers can do, Kattor," said his mother softly. "It is all I ask." And she washed him tenderly with her great rough tongue, fluffed up his bed of leaves, and purred softly to him until he went to sleep.

As Kattor grew in strength he began to compare himself with all the other animals he saw. Soon he believed there was nothing he could not conquer.

"I will conquer the world for you, Mother," said Kattor again and again.

One morning as Kattor was about to go out for his daily exercise he noticed that it was darker than usual.

"What is it, Mother?" asked Kattor.

"It is a storm," said his mother.

And just then the storm broke in all its fury. The rain came in torrents, the heavens growled like thousands of angry tigers, and trees crashed before the door of the den.

"Who is strong enough to break down trees?" asked Kattor.

"It is the wind," said his mother.

"I will conquer the wind," said Kattor, and he rushed out into the storm.

"Go away, Wind, or I will scratch you," called Kattor.

The wind only roared louder and seemed to mock him.

"Go away, Wind," cried Kattor; but his voice was drowned

by the fury of the storm.

Kattor struck again and again into the air. This was different from anything he had ever fought before. His strong paws seemed to strike nothing, and nothing fell. The wind only grew stronger and drove the rain into his eyes, and still Kattor fought, saying, "I will conquer you. I will. I will." And still the wind roared and drove rain against Kattor's body until finally he was so tired he could fight no longer.

Then, as suddenly as it had come, the storm stopped. Kattor stood still for a moment, astonished, and then ran joyfully in to see his mother.

"See, Mother, I have conquered the wind! I will conquer the world for you!"

His mother again said, "Kattor, do well the things tigers can do. Then you will always be happy." And she smoothed his fur with her great rough tongue and he slept.

When he woke up and thought of how he had driven away the rain and wind, he felt more powerful than ever.

This time he walked until he came to a great mountain.

"Get out of my way, Mountain," said Kattor.

He scratched and tore at the mountainside. His sharp claws caught in the crevices of the rocks and his paws stung with pain. It was not like the wind—it was like nothing he had tried to scratch before, but he would not give up. He scratched and scratched and tried to push the mountain with his strong head, but the mountain would not move.

And now the sun was beginning to set. It shone directly over the top of the mountain; it beat into Kattor's smarting, sand-filled eyes. Kattor could not go on, but he was determined not to be beaten. He would go home to rest and he would return in the morning, so he looked up the mountainside to where the sun shone.

"Oh, Mountain-under-the-Sun, I will conquer you in the morning," he said.

So he went home to his mother. She fed him, fluffed his bed of leaves, and with her great rough tongue she smoothed his fur and purred softly until he went to sleep.

"I *am* a great strong tiger," said Kattor as he was falling asleep, "am I not?"

"You are a strong *young* tiger," said his mother, and he slept.

The next morning he rose early to conquer the mountain. He had forgotten just where the mountain was, but he remembered that it was under the sun. Baby tiger that he was, he did not know that the evening sun (which he had seen over the mountain) was in the west, and that the morning sun (which was just rising) was in the east. So he went east instead of west.

He walked and walked and found no mountain. He walked and walked and still he found no mountain.

And then suddenly a quiver of delight ran through his yellow body from the tip of his ears to the end of his long swishy tail. He knew now! He had scared away the mountain after all. How strong and powerful he was!

He walked and walked and soon he came to more water than he had ever seen in his life before. It was the sea.

"Get out of my way, Water," said Kattor fiercely.

The water only lapped peacefully against the shore.

This made Kattor very angry. He rushed at the sea. He bit

and tore and clawed at it but he could not grasp it. No matter how hard he struck at the water, it only closed peacefully over his paws as though it could not be hurt.

Kattor, who liked to be dry and warm and comfortable, became more and more angry. Fiercer and fiercer became his blows, and still it seemed that he could not conquer the water. He fought and fought. Water got into his nose and eyes, and he was very uncomfortable. Finally, after a long time he felt that he could not go on. He wanted only to go home to his bed of warm dry leaves. He felt weak, and turning his back toward the sea, he started unsteadily for home. But what was this which greeted his eyes? Vast stretches of wet sand lay before him. He, being a baby tiger, did not know that the tide had gone out. He believed that he had chased the water far out into the sea!

"I am, after all, the most powerful tiger in the whole world," thought Kattor, and ran home to tell his mother.

"Mother," he said, breathlessly, "I conquered the wind, I frightened the mountain, and now I have scared the water away. I am a great strong tiger."

"You are still young, but you are a great strong tiger," said his mother as she washed him with her great rough tongue, and fluffed up his bed of leaves. Then she added softly as she purred him to sleep, "Tomorrow I will go with you."

And so the next day his mother went with him.

She led him up a high cliff where he had never been before. It was hard climbing, and they came to the ridge of a hill. Scarcely had Kattor put his head over the top of the hill when he felt a strong, strong breeze blowing over its edge.

"It is the wind," said Kattor's mother simply, and Kattor wondered how the wind had dared to come back. But before he was able to say anything, he saw in the distance the great mountain he thought he had frightened away.

THE STORY OF KATTOR

"It is the mountain," said Kattor's mother.

Puzzled thoughts gathered in poor Kattor's mind. Hadn't he chased the mountain and the wind away? But when he wanted to ask his mother, he found that she had wandered to the far edge of the hill and seemed to be looking away off into the distance. Kattor went to his mother, and there before him lay the water he thought he had conquered.

"It is the sea," said his mother.

Kattor did not know what to think, but his mother said nothing more, and slowly felt her way back down over the rocks.

That evening his mother fluffed up his bed and smoothed his soft fur with her great rough tongue.

"Am I *not* a great strong tiger?" asked Kattor.

"Yes, Kattor, you are a great strong tiger," said his mother gently, "but it takes more than a great strong tiger to move the winds or the mountains or the sea." And she purred softly until Kattor fell asleep.

As though in a dream, he seemed to hear her add softly, "Do well what tigers can do, Kattor. Then you will always be happy."

A Rare Provider

By Carol Ryrie Brink

IT WAS early in the winter of 1863 that Alex McCormick got as far as Dunnville in western Wisconsin with his flock of about a thousand sheep. He had intended going farther west to the open grazing land, but the roads of that time were poor, and suddenly winter had overtaken him. Snow had fallen in the morning, and now, as evening drew near, a low shaft of sunlight broke through the clouds and made broad golden bands across the snow.

Caddie Woodlawn and her younger brother, Warren, were perched on the rail fence in front of their father's farm, watching the sunset while they waited for supper. Tom, who was two years older than Caddie, stood beside them with his elbows on the top rail, and near him sat Nero, their dog.

"Red sky at night,
Sailor's delight,"

Tom said, wagging his head like a weather prophet.

"Yah," said Warren, "fair, but a lot colder tonight. I'd

hate to have to spend the night out on the road."

"Listen!" said Caddie, holding up a finger. "There's a funny noise off over the hill. Do you hear something?"

"It sounds like bells," said Warren. "We didn't miss any of the cows tonight, did we?"

"No," said Tom, "our bells don't sound like that. Besides, Nero wouldn't let a cow of ours get lost, even if *we* did." Nero usually wagged his tail appreciatively when his name was mentioned, but now his ears were cocked forward as if he, too, were listening to something far away.

"It's sheep!" said Caddie after a moment's pause. "Listen! They're all saying, 'Baa-baa—baa!' If it isn't sheep, I'll eat my best hat."

"The one with the feather?" asked Warren incredulously.

"It *must* be sheep!" said Tom.

Pouring down the road like a slow gray flood came the thousand sheep of Alex McCormick. A couple of shaggy Scotch sheep dogs ran about them, barking and keeping them on the road. They were a sorry-looking lot, tired and thin and crying from the long days of walking, and their master, who rode behind on a lame horse, was not much better. He was a tall Scotsman, his lean face browned like an Indian's. His eyes were as blue as the shadows on the snow, and they burned strangely in the dark hollows of his hungry-looking face.

"Will ye tell your daddy I'd like to speak wi' him?" he called

as he came abreast of the three children.

Tom dashed away, with a whoop, for Father. Soon the whole Woodlawn household had turned out to witness the curious sight of nearly a thousand weary sheep milling about in the open space before the farm. They had cows and horses and oxen, but none of the pioneer farmers in the valley had yet brought in sheep.

Caddie and Warren stood up on the top rail, balancing themselves precariously and trying to count the sheep. Nero circled about, uncertain whether or not to be friendly with the strange dogs, and deeply suspicious of the plaintive bleatings and baaings of the sheep.

Suddenly Caddie hopped off the fence in the midst of the sheep.

"Look, mister! There's something wrong with this one." One of the ewes had dropped down in her tracks and looked as if she might be dying. But Mr. McCormick and Father were deep in conversation and paid no attention to her.

"Here, Caddie! Tom! Warren!" called Father. "We've got to help Mr. McCormick find shelter for his sheep tonight. Run to the neighbors and ask them if they can spare some barn or pasture room and come and help us."

The three children started off across the fields in different directions. As she raced across the light snow toward the Silvernail's farm, Caddie saw tracks ahead of her. Topping the first rise, she saw her little sister Hetty already on her way to tell Lida Silvernail. Hetty's bonnet and her red knitted mittens flew behind her by their strings, for Hetty never bothered with her bonnet or mittens when there was news to be spread. So Caddie veered north toward the Seevers.

Although Alex McCormick was a stranger to them all, the men from the neighboring farms had soon gathered to help him save his weary sheep from the cold. With a great deal of shouting, barking, and bleating, the flock was divided into small sections and driven off to different farms, where the sheep could shelter under haystacks or sheds through the cold night.

When the last sheep were being driven off, Caddie remembered the sick ewe and ran to see what had become of her. She still lay where she had fallen, her eyes half closed, her breath coming so feebly that it seemed as if she scarcely lived at all.

"Oh, look, Mr. McCormick!" called Caddie. "You ought to tend to this one or she'll be a goner."

"Hoot!" said the Scotsman. "I've no time to waste on a dead one with hundreds of live ones still on their legs and like to freeze to death the night."

"I've got lots of time, if you haven't, Mr. McCormick," volunteered Caddie.

"Verra good," said the Scotsman. "I'll give her to ye, lassie, if ye can save her life."

"Really?" cried Caddie. "It's a bargain!" In a moment she had enlisted the services of Tom and Warren, and they were staggering along under the dead weight of the helpless sheep. Their father watched them with a twinkle of amusement in his eye.

"And what are you going to do with that?" he asked.

"It's nothing but a sick sheep," said Tom, "but Caddie thinks she can save it."

"Oh, Father," cried Caddie, "may I put her in the box stall and give her something to eat?

She's just worn out."

Father nodded and smiled.

"I'll look around at her later," he said.

But when Father found time later to visit the box stall, he found Caddie sitting with a lantern beside her ewe and looking very disconsolate.

"Father, I know she's hungry, but I can't make her eat. I don't know what to do."

Mr. Woodlawn knelt beside the animal and felt her all over for possible injuries. Then he opened her mouth and ran his fingers gently over her gums.

"Well, Caddie," he said, "I guess you'll have to make her a set of false teeth."

"False teeth!" echoed Caddie. Then she stuck her own fingers in the ewe's mouth. "She hasn't any teeth!" she cried. "No wonder she couldn't chew hay! Whatever shall we do?"

Mr. Woodlawn looked thoughtfully into his small daughter's worried face.

"Well," he said, "it would be quite a task, and I don't know whether you want to undertake it."

"Yes, I do," said Caddie. "Tell me what."

"Mother has more of those small potatoes than she can use this winter. Get her to cook some of them for you until they are quite soft, and mix them with bran and milk into a mash. I think you can pull your old sheep through on that. But it will be an every day job. You'll find it pretty tiresome."

"Oh! But, Father, it's better than having her die!"

That evening Mr. McCormick stayed for supper with the Woodlawn family. With Father and Mother at each end of the table, with the six children ranged around, and Robert Ireton, the hired man, and Katie Conroy, the hired girl, there, too—they made an appreciative audience. Mr. McCormick's tongue with its rich Scotch burr was loosened to relate for them the story of his long journey from the East with his sheep. He told how Indians had stolen some and wolves others; how the herdsman he had brought with him had caught a fever and died on the way, and was buried at the edge of an Indian village; how they had forded streams and weathered a tornado.

While the dishes were being cleared away, the Scotsman took Hetty and little Minnie on his knees and told them about the thatched home in Scotland where he had been born. Then he opened a wallet which he had inside his buckskin shirt, to show them some treasure which he kept there. They all crowded around to see. It was a bit of dried heather which had come from Scotland.

As the stranger talked, Caddie's mind kept going to the barn, and something warm and pleasant sang inside her.

"She ate the potato mash," she thought. "If I take good care of her, she'll live, and it will be all because of me! I love her more than any pet I've got—except, of course, Nero."

The next day, Mr. McCormick set out for Dunnville to try to sell as many of his sheep as he could. Winter had overtaken him too soon, and after all his long journey he found himself still far from open grazing land and without sheds or shelter to keep the sheep over the winter. But Dunnville was a small place, and he could sell only a very small part of his huge flock. When he had disposed of all he could, he made an agreement with Mr. Woodlawn and the other farmers that they might keep as many of his sheep as they could feed and shelter over the winter, if they would give him half of the wool and half of the lambs in the spring.

"How about mine?" asked Caddie. Mr. McCormick laughed.

"Nay, lassie," he said. "You've earned the old ewe fair an' square, and everything that belongs to her."

The old ewe was on her feet now, and baaing and nuzzling Caddie's hand whenever Caddie came near her. That was a busy winter for Caddie. Before school in the morning and after school in the evening, there were always mashes of vegetables and bran to be cooked up for Nanny.

"You'll get tired of doing that," said Tom.

"Nanny!" scoffed Warren. "That's a name for a goat."

"No," said Caddie firmly. "That's a name for Caddie Woodlawn's sheep, and you see if I get tired of feeding her!"

When the days began to lengthen and grow warmer toward the end of February, Caddie turned Nanny out during the day with the other sheep. At first she tied a red woolen string about Nanny's neck, for sheep are very much alike, and Caddie did not want to lose her own. But really that was quite unnecessary for, as soon as Nanny saw her coming with a pan of mash and an iron spoon, she broke away from the others and made a beeline for Caddie. At night she came to the barn and waited for Caddie to let her in.

One morning in March, when Caddie had risen early to serve Nanny's breakfast before she went to school, Robert came out of the barn to meet her. She had flung Mother's shawl on over her pinafore, and the pan of warm mash which she carried steamed cozily in the chill spring air.

For once Robert was neither singing nor whistling at his work. He looked at Caddie with such a mixture of sorrow and glad tidings on his honest Irish face that Caddie stopped short.

"Something's happened!" she cried.

"Aye. Faith, an' you may well say so, Miss Caddie," said Robert seriously.

Caddie's heart almost stopped beating for a moment. Something had happened to Nanny! She ran into the barn.

"You're not to feel too grieved now, Mavoureen," said Robert, coming after her. "You did more for the poor beast than any other body would have done."

But words meant nothing to Caddie now, for the thin thread of life which she had coaxed along in the sick sheep all winter had finally ebbed away, and Nanny was dead. Caddie flung away the mash and knelt down beside the old sheep. She could not speak or make a sound, but the hot tears ran down her cheeks and tasted salty on her lips. Her heart felt ready to burst with sorrow.

"Wurra! Wurra! Wurra!" said Robert sympathetically, leaning over the side of the stall and looking down on them. "But 'tis an ill wind that blows nobody good. Why don't ye look around an' see the good the ill wind has been a-blowing of you?"

Caddie shook her head, squeezing her eyes tight shut to keep the tears from flowing so fast.

"Look!" he urged again.

Robert had come into the stall and thrust something soft and warm under her hand. The something soft and warm stirred, and a faint small voice said, "Ma-a-a!"

"Look!" said Robert. "Its ma is dead, and, faith, if 'tis not a-callin' *you* ma! It knows which side its bread is buttered on."

Caddie opened her eyes. Her tears had ceased to flow, for Robert had put into her arms something so young and so lovable that half of her sorrow was already swept away.

"It's a lamb!" said Caddie, half to herself, and then to Robert, "Is it—Nanny's?"

"Aye," said Robert, "it is that. But Nanny was too tired to mother it. 'Sure, an' 'tis all right for me to go to sleep and leave it,' says Nanny, 'for Caddie Woodlawn is a rare provider!' "

Caddy wrapped the shawl around her baby and cradled the small shivering creature in her arms.

"Potato mash won't do," she was saying to herself. "Warm milk is what it needs, and maybe Mother will give me one of baby Joe's bottles to make the feeding easier."

The lamb cuddled warmly and closely against her. "Ma-a-a-a!" it said.

From *Magical Melons*

Meals for Mickey

By Alice Dalgliesh

IT'S too hot to do anything," said Tim. He ran his hands through his wet, fair hair until it stood on end.

"But think how much hotter it is in the city," said Robin. "In our apartment it must be simply sizzling."

Tim and his sister were sitting on the hill looking down over their house. It was a small white house, snuggled close on the Connecticut hillside, a comfortable little house with a gray roof and climbing roses over the doorways. It had not belonged to the Storms long enough for them to be quite used to it; in fact, they had bought it only three months before. Inside the house there was still a great deal to be done; it was an old house and had not been lived in for years.

"Mother wants us to help her take the old wallpaper off our room," said Robin. "She said we could wait a day or two until it was cooler."

"I should think so!" said Tim. He looked down at the little village that lay in the valley, far below their own house. A bright red roof stood out among the gray ones.

"Look, Robin! That's the new hot-dog stand. Let's go down and get a frozen custard. Haven't you a nickel?"

"Yes," said Robin, "but I was going to buy—"

"Oh, come on—it's too hot to do anything else. We'll stop

and ask Mother if we can go."

A few minutes later Tim and Robin were on their way down the sunny road. As they reached the highway, a long string of cars went hurrying past, cars of people trying to escape the city heat. In front of the hot-dog stand many cars were parked. Under a large tree there were several tables. One was vacant.

"Let's eat out here instead of having a cone," said Robin. They sat down and soon were eating the cold frozen custard.

"M—m! This is the stuff," said Tim. "Make it last a long time, Robin."

Robin took a quarter of a spoonful. Then she dropped her spoon in the dish.

"Tim, look! LOOK!"

An enormous, tan-colored dog was coming through the doorway of the little house. Slowly it walked over to the table where the children sat. For a moment it stood looking at them, then came forward and stood beside Robin, wagging its tail.

"It's a Great Dane!" said Robin. She patted the huge head. "He's friendly."

The woman who kept the stand came out. "Don't you want a dog?" she asked.

Robin and Tim stared at her, wondering if they had heard the words aright.

"A dog? Not *this* one?"

The woman nodded. "Yes. I haven't had him long. His master moved away and couldn't take him so he gave him to us. Since we've had the stand, he's been a pest. He's scared of motorcycles—shivers when he hears one. And he frightens the customers. Gentle as a kitten he is, but how would they know that?"

Robin looked at Tim. "Can we take him? Shall we go home and ask Mother first?"

"If we do," said Tim, "she'll say 'no.' But if we walk into the yard with a perfectly beautiful dog, she won't have the heart to refuse. Let's try it, anyway."

"You'll have no trouble holding him," said the woman, as she snapped the leash on the big dog's collar. "He's trained to walk by you and not tug at the leash."

"What is his name?" asked Robin. Her answer made both children laugh and they were still giggling as they went up the road. They took turns holding the leash, and the big dog paced alongside them like a gentleman.

Mother was in the garden when the children and the dog turned in the gate.

"Mother," said Tim, with a confidence he did not really feel. "This is our new dog."

"Well, really!" said Mother. "Nothing much surprises me any more, but this is difficult. Suppose you explain!"

It took quite a bit of explaining. Mother looked doubtful. The children looked worried. Then the dog walked up to Mother and rubbed his head against her.

"He's pretty nice," admitted Mother. "What is his name?"

"Mickey Mouse!" said Robin in a slightly choked voice, and all three of them laughed until they ached.

"Mickey Mouse!" said Mother. "It simply *can't* be. I think

I'll say you can keep him if you change his name. A Great Dane named Mickey Mouse is just *too* much."

"We could call him Sir Michael," said Robin. "Mickey for short."

"Hooray! We can keep him!" shouted Tim. "Mom, you're a good sport!"

"Of course there's Father to be thought of, too," said Mother. "It's time to go meet the 5:55—so let's all go to the station and break the news."

Father took the news calmly, but said just one thing that disturbed everyone.

"My dear young friends," he said, "have you remembered that your father is an artist and that sometimes he makes money and sometimes not? And have you thought of how much food a Great Dane eats in one day? Can't you guess?"

"How much?" asked Robin anxiously.

"Four pounds of meat," answered Father. There was dead silence. Everyone knew about the price of meat, and since they had bought the house there had not been much extra money.

"We'll have to do something to earn the money," said Tim. "We'll have to keep him. Perhaps I could mow lawns."

"We'll think it over," said Father. "Remember you're not so good even at mowing our own lawn. Anyway, we'd better stop at the store and get the animal some food. We can't let him starve to death."

The Storms all sat around and watched Mickey have his first meal. It was all over in an astonishingly short time.

"If only his mouth were smaller, or something," said Robin. "It's like the Mammoth Cave of Kentucky."

"That wouldn't help. It's his stomach that's too big," said Tim. "I've read that if you don't eat for days your stomach shrinks. Maybe we could shrink his."

"Not a chance," said Father, gloomily.

Night came and with it the question of a bed for Mickey. Mickey himself settled it, for he stretched out on the rug in front of the fire.

"He looks as if he'd always been here!" said Tim. "I guess dogs know when people really want them."

The next day the Storms began to find out that having a Great Dane in a small house is like having an elephant in a too small enclosure. One had to get used to Mickey.

In the afternoon a friend of Mother's came to visit, a friend who owned a very small Pomeranian called "Ducky." Tim and Robin called him "the puffball," and did not consider him a dog at all. Somehow, when the puffball arrived, Mother forgot about Mickey. Ducky was prancing about the lawn looking like an animated powder puff when Mickey came round the corner. Ducky's mistress screamed. Mother and children sat in frozen horror. Ducky stood still and Mickey bore down upon him.

A thought flashed through Robin's mind. "Mickey's mouth! The puffball will make exactly one mouthful." But Mickey's mouth did not open. The puffball stood his ground. Mickey's great tail began to wag. The dogs met. They sniffed. The puffball's tail began to wag. Away over the lawn went the two dogs, the puffball yelping joyously.

"I'll never laugh at Ducky again," whispered Robin to Tim.

MEALS FOR MICKEY

"He ought to have a medal or something for standing still and letting a great giant like that come up to him."

The first week went by without any mishaps except that Mickey lay down in the middle of one of Mother's pet garden beds, and when he got up, there was a very large, flat place.

"He has only to lie down a few more times," said Mother, "and there will be no garden at all." She looked at the flattened zinnias. "A steam roller couldn't have done better."

It was a little unfortunate, perhaps, that the grocery bill came in on the day that Mickey had sat down in the garden. "Look at it," said Mother.

"4 pounds of hamburger—for Mickey.

"6 lamb chops—those were for us.

"4 pounds of hamburger—for Mickey.

"1 sirloin roast—for us.

"And so on. Mickey eats more than we do! Something must be done about it." Mother was very emphatic.

That night Robin and Tim went to bed feeling very sad indeed. After they were in bed, they could hear Father and Mother talking. Bits of conversation floated in to them: "—can't possibly do it"—"another home"—"perhaps on a farm"—"the children will be upset." Robin cried herself to sleep.

The next day the weather was cooler than it had been for some time, and the children began work on the wallpaper of their room. Mickey lay watching them, his head on his paws. Already, he found his new home very satisfactory.

"Robin," said Tim as he peeled a long strip of wallpaper,

"Mother didn't say anything about Mickey this morning, did she? Do you think she's changed her mind?"

"I'm afraid not," sighed Robin. "O Tim, what do you suppose that funny bulge is over the fireplace?"

Tim came over to look. "It's something they used to close up the stove hole," he said.

Robin went on peeling and scraping. "Tim! It's canvas! It looks like the back of a picture."

"Sure does!" said Tim. "They've got an old piece of canvas or else a painting tacked over there. Easy, Robin! I'll get the screw driver."

Carefully they pried the canvas loose from the wall. It was sooty and dusty, but it was a picture.

"Mother!" they shouted, "come quickly! Look what we found." Mother came hurrying in. She looked at the picture carefully, took a rag, and removed some of the dirt.

"It's an old portrait of a child," she said. "It might be valuable, and we'd better wait for Father. He will know just how to clean it up."

"Valuable!" Robin and Tim looked at each other, the same thought racing through their minds. Perhaps it would mean at least a dozen square meals for Mickey!

Father was even more excited about the picture than the rest of the family had been. He cleaned it carefully. It was a portrait of a little fair-haired girl in a stiff, brocaded dress.

"It must be quite old," said Robin.

"The face looks as if it didn't belong to the rest of it."

"It doesn't," said Father. "Traveling portrait painters used to paint the bodies and clothes of their pictures in the wintertime, then in the summer the pictures were all ready to have the faces painted in. Of course the clothes didn't really suit the people who had the portraits painted. This little girl probably never wore such a handsome dress."

"How queer!" said Tim. "But, do you think it's valuable?"

"I'm pretty sure it is," said Father. He looked at the large blank space over the big living-room fireplace. "It would go well there."

Tim and Robin looked at each other in despair.

"We thought—" began Robin.

"We hoped—" went on Tim.

"That we could sell the picture," said Robin. "The money would feed Mickey for at least a week."

"We must think this over," said Father. "You found it, but I paid for the house. So the picture is partly mine, isn't it?"

"I suppose so," said Tim slowly. "Then we ought to share the proceeds."

"That's the right way of it," said Father. "I tell you what we'll do. I'll agree that if the picture is really valuable, one half of the money shall go to feed Mickey for as long as it lasts and one half shall be used on house improvements."

The children agreed that this was fair. Father rolled the picture up carefully and took it into town with him. The day seemed long, and the children got Mother and the car to the 5:55 fifteen minutes ahead of time. They walked slowly up and down the platform, with Mickey pacing behind them. Mickey was feeling snug and comfortable inside, for he had just finished four pounds of hamburger. He knew, however, that something must be wrong, so he tried licking their hands to see if that would help. It did not seem to help very much. Tears came into Robin's eyes and splashed on Mickey's head as she put her arm around his neck.

"You're such a lamb, Mickey, suppose the picture isn't worth much and we can't keep you?"

The train was coming down the track. It stopped and Father got off. Two children and a dog rushed up to him so fast that Father almost lost his balance.

"Steady! Steady there!"

"Father—is it?"

"Can we?"

"Was it—"

"It was," said Father as they got into the car. "Quite valuable, though not so valuable as I expected. Anyway, your share will be enough to keep Mickey for a year—maybe longer. I also went to see a man who raises dogs and he told me about a good kennel food that's cheaper than meat. There's just one thing," he stopped and looked seriously at the children. "I am starting a bank account for you, and you may draw out enough for Mickey's food each month. But—what about the time when Robin wants a new book, or Tim wants something for his bicycle? What about ice-cream cones?"

By this time the car had turned in the gate and stopped in front of the door. Mickey was bounding joyfully across the lawn as if he knew that this was his home forever. Robin looked down across the valley. The red roof of the hot-dog stand seemed very inviting. But Robin shook her head.

"No," she said. "Not one penny goes for anything but hamburger and dog food. And when it's all used up, we'll find a way to get some more. Mickey is going to stay!"

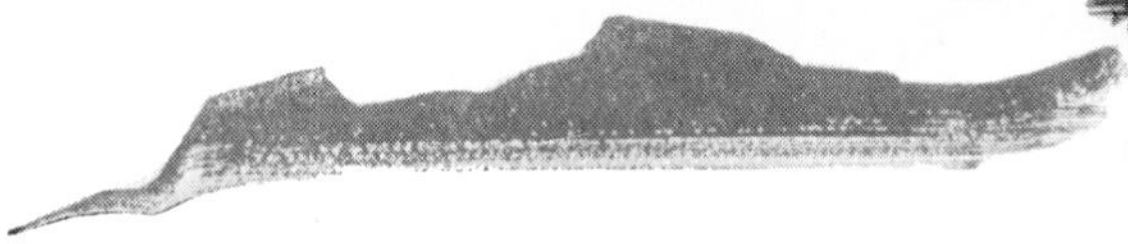

The Pulling Bee

By Marguerite Henry

ONE afternoon early in May, Joel stood looking out the door of the inn where he was serving as an apprentice. Suddenly the yard began filling with big-faced dray horses, and oxen and men were gathering about a huge pine log.

"Is it a pulling bee?" asked Joel, turning to Mister Chase, the owner of the inn.

"If Nathan Nye is about, looking important, you can expect most anything. He was ever good at fixing contests."

"He's there!" exclaimed Joel. "And he's got tug chains."

"H'm," mused Mr. Chase, smiling at his young apprentice, "if I was a boy now with no chores to do, it seems like I'd skedaddle right out there."

Joel grinned, and in no time at all was helping Mister Nye fasten the tug chains to Lucy, a big dappled mare.

The mare's owner, Abel Hooper, was too busy boasting to be of any help. "A mighty lucky thing I'm first," he was saying. "Lucy and me'll pull this here piece o' kindling to the sawmill in one pull. Then you can all go home whilst it's still daylight."

But Lucy barely caused the log to tremble.

One after another, the beasts had their turn, and no matter how whips cracked or masters yelled, the log seemed rooted to the earth.

"Folks, I guess it's up to the oxen now," Nathan Nye was saying, when into the yard came Evans riding Little Bub, the horse which he had rented for a year. Joel had gentled Bub, and a staunch friendship had grown up between the boy and the little horse.

"Hey, Nathan," called Evans, "what's all the hullabaloo?"

"'Tis a pulling bee," answered Mister Nye, "but can't none of the beasts pull that there pine log to the sawmill in three pulls or less. Just look at Hooper's big mare! She's roaring from the try. And Biggle's gelding—his muscles are still a-hitching and a-twitching. Even Ezra Wiggins' beast failed. None of them can budge the log."

"None except my one-horse team!" crowed Evans.

Joel held his breath. He felt scared right down to his toes. The crowd snickered. Then it hooted.

"*That* little flea? Why, he's just a sample of a horse. He ain't no bigger than a mouse's whisker! Besides, his tail is so long, he's liable to get all tangled up and break a leg."

THE PULLING BEE

Evans looked over the horseflesh. "Little Bub," he said slowly, "ain't exactly what you'd call a dray horse, but whatever he's hitched to generally has to come the first time trying."

"Take him on home," scoffed Nathan Nye. "When we have a contest for ponies, we'll be letting you know."

Above the man-talk Joel heard the sharp voice of Mistress Chase. "Boy! You come here!"

On his way in, Joel stopped only long enough to press his face hard against Little Bub's nose.

At the door Mistress Chase handed him a kettle of hasty pudding and a long stick.

"Hang the kettle over the fire," she said, "and stir and stir until I tell you to quit."

"Hasty pudding!" muttered Joel to himself. "It beats me how it got its name!"

Evans strutted into the room just then. "Chase!" he called to the innkeeper. "I've got a horse that can move that pine log to the sawmill in two pulls. But first, pour me a mugful of cider. I'm dying of thirst."

At sound of Evans' voice Joel almost upset the pudding.

"Boy!" shrilled Mistress Chase. "Mind your work. Hasty pudding's not meant to feed the fire!"

For once Joel paid no heed. He tore across the room and grabbed Mister Evans by the sleeve.

"Mister Evans!" he cried. "Little Bub's been dragging logs

all day. You hain't going to enter him in the pulling bee?"

Evans gulped his drink. "Go away, Joel," he snapped. "When I want advice, I'll not ask it of a whippersnapper."

The little horse meanwhile was feasting upon all the fresh green shoots within his range. They tasted juicy and delicious after the business of logging.

One by one the stars dusted the sky. Nathan Nye brought out a lanthorn so Mister Evans could see to fasten his tug-chains to the log.

Joel followed Evans about like a puppy. Evans stood it as long as he could. Finally he shoved the boy aside.

"A nettle hain't half as pesky as you," he growled. "Stand back or I'll clout you."

Now Evans was stepping off the ten rods to the mill.

"Want to give up before you start?" scoffed Nathan Nye.

"No such a thing. Why, I'm actually ashamed to ask my horse to pull such a little log. Now if you'll find me three stout men to sit astride the log, why then I'll ask him."

Joel bit his lips to keep from crying out. He hid his face in the horse's tangled mane. "Oh, Bub, my poor little Bub," he choked, "none of the big creatures could budge the log, and now with three men besides. Oh Bub, Bub . . ."

Laughter rang up and down the valley. "Ho-ho-ho—that pint-sized cob to pull such a big log! Ho-ho . . ."

Nathan Nye had no trouble at all in finding three brawny volunteers. As the men straddled the log, they joked and laughed and poked one another in the ribs.

"Look to your feet, men!" warned Evans. "This horse means business. Something's got to give."

Nye held the lanthorn aloft. It lighted the circle of faces. They were tense with excitement. Some of the men were whittling like mad. Joel was white with anger.

Nye repeated the warning. "Look to your feet, men!"

Evans felt to see

if the horse was hitched securely. Then, "Git up!" he roared, as he slashed the whip across Bub's back.

The little horse galvanized into action. First, he backed ever so slightly. Then his powerful neck bent low, as if to give every muscle a chance. Now he was straining forward. You could see his muscles grow firm and swell up like rubber balls. You could see the white foam come out on his body.

Joel, too, was drenched in sweat. The silence was heavy, like a gray blanket.

At last there was the groaning of chains. The log trembled. Slowly it moved. It kept on moving. It was more than halfway to the saw!

The little horse stopped. His sides were heaving. Joel breathed in and out with the horse. He felt as if his lungs were on fire. There was no sound at all from the crowd.

Now Evans commanded again. And again the horse went through the same motions. He backed slightly. He bent his head. He strained every muscle. Again the log was moving, moving, moving. This time it did not stop until it reached the sawmill!

And still nobody had made a sound. The three men were as silent as the log they sat upon. Only the horse's breathing pierced the quiet.

Then everyone began shouting at once. "Hooray for Morgan's colt! Hooray! Hooray! Hooray for the big-little horse."

Joel had his arms around Bub's neck. His whole body ached, as if he had moved the log himself. "It's over! It's over! You did it, Bub! You did it!" he kept repeating. Then he sobbed a little from exhaustion and relief.

The horse lipped Joel's cheek and neck. He almost tried to say, "It's all right, Joel; don't be taking it so hard." He was steaming and tired, but it was good to be near the boy again. It was good. He nickered softly.

From *Justin Morgan Had a Horse*

Johnny and His Mule

By Ellis Credle

AWAY up in the Great Smoky Mountains there is a town which is called Horn Hollow. It is not a very large town and the great mountains standing up all around make it seem very small indeed. There are no more than twenty dwellings there, a courthouse, several stores, a church, and a schoolhouse.

To this little schoolhouse long ago came all the children in the town and a little mountain boy named Johnny. Johnny lived far back in the hills, a long, long way from town. He had to get up very early, when the chickens were just crowing for the sunrise, to get to school on time. But in spite of the long walk over the mountains he was never late.

The town children might bustle into the schoolyard as the last bell was ringing, they might catch the end of the line as it was marching into the school, they might even tiptoe fearfully into the room after classes had started—but never Johnny! He was always in his place as the line marched in and in his proper seat when classes began. In the fall, in the winter, and in the spring, it was always the same. Johnny was always on time!

But one day, toward the end of the school year, Johnny was late! The last bell rang—Johnny was not there! Nine o'clock came—and still no Johnny. Ten o'clock rolled around, half-past ten, and not a sign of Johnny. It was so very late now, the children and the teacher began to wonder what had happened. Perhaps Johnny was sick, or perhaps he had fallen over the steep mountainside on the way to school. But a half hour later, at eleven o'clock, there was a shuffle-shuffle-shuffle outside the door. It opened slowly and Johnny creaked guiltily into the room.

"Why, Johnny!" cried the teacher. "It's eleven o'clock! Why are you so late?"

"I just couldn't help it, Miss Mary!" stammered Johnny, and he looked as though he might cry at any moment.

"But tell me, what happened?" urged Miss Mary.

"I got into town early this morning, Miss Mary," began Johnny, "in plenty of time for school, but I stopped for a minute in the town square to watch the auction sale."

Everyone knew about the auction. It was held every Friday and the mountaineers called it "Trade Day." They came in from the surrounding hills and ranges, bringing anything which they wanted to swap or sell. Handmade chairs, baskets, turkeys, jackknives, horses, preserves, feather pillows, anything and everything went on sale in the town square on Friday.

"And so," continued Johnny, "while I was standing there, an old mule was put up to be sold. The auctioneer began shouting, 'What am I offered for this mule? What am I bid?'

"Nobody would begin the bidding, and so, just to get the sale

started, I hollered out, 'I bid five cents!' I thought sure somebody would bid higher, because mules usually cost a lot of money. But nobody did, and so they gave me the mule!

"And there I stood, Miss Mary, holding the mule by the halter. I didn't know what to do with him! About the only thing I could think of was to take him along to school with me. So I started toward the schoolhouse leading the mule.

"I soon found out why nobody wanted that mule at any price. After we had gone about a block he stopped stock-still. I tried every way to get him to go along but he wouldn't budge an inch! He was a balker! Lots of other people tried to make him go, but no, sir! That mule wouldn't go until he felt like it! After awhile he walked another block and then he balked again. Miss Mary, it took me two hours to get that critter four blocks to the schoolhouse! That's why I'm late, honest to goodness!"

"Why, Johnny!" exclaimed Miss Mary, "I never heard such a tale!"

"If you don't believe it, Miss Mary, just look out the window," replied Johnny.

The teacher gazed through the window and so did all the pupils. There tied to a tree was a mule. His head hung down and his large ears flopped sadly over his face. There was no doubt about it, Johnny's tale was true.

When the bell rang for closing time all the children rushed

into the schoolyard and gathered around the mule, laughing and joking and poking fun at Johnny and his animal.

"Such a sad-looking critter! What are you going to do with him, Johnny?" asked his little friend Matthey.

Johnny did not feel very gay. "I don't know what to do with him," he said wretchedly. "If it took me two hours to get him a few blocks to school, how long will it take me to get him home? It will be black night and the owls a-hooting before I could get him halfway there!"

Johnny leaned against the tree beside his mule and began to cry. The children stopped laughing and looked at each other.

"Hold on there, Johnny, you never can tell about a balking mule," comforted Matthey. "He may be ready to go by now. Maybe he'll start right off!"

Johnny brightened up. "Maybe he will!" he said. He untied the mule's rope and tried to lead him forward. But the mule was *not* ready to go and he did *not* start right off. Johnny braced himself and pulled. But the mule was not in the notion.

"Give me a handhold and I'll help you pull," said Matthey.

"I'll help too," said Nancy-Belle. Both children threw their weight against the mule. But he did not budge.

"Move up a little and we'll pull too," said Lem and Hezekiah.

"We'll all pull!" said Hetty and Hank and Jonas. They grasped the mule's halter and hauled with all their might. But the mule only braced himself and stood in his tracks.

While the children were pulling and straining and puffing and blowing, the teacher came out of the schoolhouse.

"What's the matter?" she called. "Can't you get the mule to start?"

"No, ma'am, he won't seem to go!" they all cried.

"Here, let me get a hold. I'll pull too!" said Miss Mary. But one more made no difference to the mule. His mind was made up.

"Maybe we ought to try something else," said the teacher.

They all let go of the halter and mopped their foreheads.

"My father once had a balking mule," piped up Nancy-Belle, "and he used to get him to go by patting him in the breast."

"Yes, I've heard of that, too," agreed Lem. "Lots of balkers will go if you just pat them in the breast."

And so Johnny stepped up under the mule's chin and patted him gently on the breast. The mule did not budge.

"Pat him a little harder," urged Nancy-Belle, "maybe he didn't feel that!"

Johnny slapped the mule again, smartly this time, clap-clap-clap! When the animal made no move to start, Johnny whacked him with all his might, smack-smack-smack! The mule only rolled his eyes and wiggled his ears. It was plain to see that patting on the breast had not put him in the notion to go.

"My uncle once had a balking mule," offered Hetty. "He used to get behind him with a plank and push him."

"That's right," added Hank. "They used to push the mule a few steps forward. After that he would go all by himself."

"Maybe that's just what this mule needs," said Miss Mary. "Where can we find a plank?"

The children hustled around and underneath the edge of the schoolhouse they found a long piece of plank. They put it behind the mule's haunches and pushed. They huffed and they puffed but the mule stood pat!

The children stopped for breath.

"Maybe the mule is hungry," spoke up Nancy-Belle. "If we got a piece of corn and held it out to him, maybe he'd follow."

Johnny ran to the nearest house and brought back an ear of

corn. He held it out to the mule. Yes, the mule was hungry. He stretched his neck toward the corn.

The children held their breath. The mule took one step forward. Johnny backed away, holding the corn just out of reach. The mule took another step forward, then another and another. A loud shout rose from the children. "Hurrah! Hurrah! He's going!" they yelled.

The teacher held the mule's halter while Johnny danced ahead with the corn. Through the town they went clip-clop, clip-clop. Over the mountain trail they started as fast as they could go. But still Johnny did not seem very happy.

"A balking mule is no good to anybody," he grieved. "I'm afraid my Pappy will be as mad as fire when he sees this critter. Like as not he'll give me a good licking."

"No use borrowing trouble," said the teacher. "Let's sing a song and forget all about the mule."

Johnny struck up an old

LOUIS DECHMAN

mountain hunting song and along they went singing:

Jay-bird settin' on a hick'ry limb,
Hi, ho, diddle dum dee-ay!
My rifle-gun'll shore git him!
Hi, ho, diddle dum dee-ay!
My true love lives up the river,
Hi, ho, diddle dum dee-ay!
A few more jumps and I'll be with 'er
Hi, ho, diddle dum dee-ay!

After that Johnny felt better. But the mule did not care for anything except the ear of corn that was always just out of reach. He kept his eyes glued upon it and went prancing along, clippity-clop, clippity-clop!

As they came nearer and nearer home, Johnny began to worry again. "Another thing about a balking mule," he said, "he's always hungry. Why, this old mule could eat us out of house and home in no time! I'm a-going to get that licking as sure as shooting!" He dreaded to reach home.

But the mule took them there in short order. Johnny's Mammy and Pappy were sitting on the front step.

When they saw Johnny and the teacher and the mule, their eyes almost popped out of their heads.

"Well dog-gone my time! What's this turning in at the front gate?" exclaimed Pappy.

"It's a mule, a balking mule!" blurted Johnny. "I bought him at the auction for five cents!"

"My stars and stockings!" cried Mammy. "What on earth can we do with a balking mule?"

Pappy did not say anything. He only rubbed his chin and looked doubtfully at the animal.

The sun was setting by this time. It was much too late for the teacher to return to town. She spent the night with Johnny's

parents. They entertained her with true mountain hospitality. There was fried chicken that night for supper and hot biscuits and cold buttermilk. For dessert there was yellow honey from their own beehives, and a pot full of pungent sassafras tea.

After supper everyone sat around the fire, which leaped brightly in the old stone fireplace. Pappy got out his zither and played a soft tinkling accompaniment while Mammy sang some old, old mountain ballads for the teacher.

Johnny sat in the chimney corner. He did not feel very happy because he kept wondering if his Pappy felt angry about the mule. At last he screwed up his courage.

"Pappy," he said timidly, "that balking mule is going to be sort of a nuisance, I reckon."

"Nuisance!" cried Pappy. "Why, I know how to make that old mule do all my ploughing and hauling and turning of my sorghum mill!" He winked at Miss Mary, "I know a little trick that will make a balking mule work harder than a hornet!"

"What's that?" cried Johnny and Miss Mary in a breath.

"Wait until the morning," laughed Pappy. "Look out the window when you first wake up and you'll find out!"

The teacher went to bed in the spare room and Johnny climbed the ladder to his little room in the loft. In the morning he woke up early and looked out the window. There, pulling a plough briskly through the corn patch, was the balking mule. Hanging on to the handles of the plough was Pappy. He looked up and caught sight of Johnny.

"He's a fine strong mule!" cried Pappy. "I'm much obliged to you!"

But the mule did not look up, nor to the right nor to the left. He was gazing greedily straight ahead at the ear of corn that dangled in front of his nose!

From *Uncle Sam's Story Book*

How the Camel Got His Hump

BY RUDYARD KIPLING

IN THE beginning of years, when the world was so new and all, and the Animals were just beginning to work for Man, there was a Camel, and he lived in the middle of a Howling Desert because he did not want to work; and besides, he was a Howler himself. So he ate sticks and thorns and tamarisks and milkweed and prickles, most 'scruciating idle; and when anybody spoke to him he said, "Humph!" Just "Humph!" and no more.

Presently the Horse came to him on Monday morning, with a saddle on his back and a bit in his mouth, and said, "Camel, O Camel, come out and trot like the rest of us."

"Humph!" said the Camel, and the Horse went away and told the Man.

Presently the Dog came to him, with a stick in his mouth, and said, "Camel, O Camel, come and fetch and carry like the rest of us."

"Humph!" said the Camel; and the Dog went away and told the Man.

Presently the Ox came to him, with the yoke on his neck and said, "Camel, O Camel, come and plow like the rest of us."

"Humph!" said the Camel, and the Ox went away and told the Man.

At the end of the day the Man called the Horse and the Dog and the Ox together, and said, "Three, O Three, I'm very sorry for you (with the world so new-and-all); but that Humph-thing in the Desert can't work, or he would have been here by now, so I am going to leave him alone, and you must work double time to make up for it."

That made the Three very angry (with the world so new-and-all), and they held a palaver, and an *indaba,* and a *punchayet,* and a powwow on the edge of the Desert; and the Camel came chewing milkweed *most* 'scruciating idle, and laughed at them. Then he said "Humph!" and went away again.

Presently there came along the Djinn in charge of All Deserts, rolling in a cloud of dust (Djinns always travel that way because it is Magic), and he stopped to palaver and powwow with the Three.

"Djinn of All Deserts," said the Horse, "is it right for any one to be idle, with the world so new-and-all?"

"Certainly not," said the Djinn.

"Well," said the Horse, "there's a thing in the middle of your Howling Desert (and he's a Howler himself) with a long neck and long legs, and he hasn't done a stroke of work since Monday morning. He won't trot."

"Whew!" said the Djinn, whistling, "that's my Camel, for all the gold in Arabia! What does he say about it?"

He says, 'Humph!'" said the Dog, "and he won't fetch and carry."

"Does he say anything else?"

"Only 'Humph!', and he won't plow," said the Ox.

"Very good," said the Djinn. "I'll 'humph' him if you will kindly wait a minute."

The Djinn rolled himself up in his dustcloak, and took a bearing across the desert, and found the Camel most 'scruciatingly idle, looking at his own reflection in a pool of water.

"My long and bubbling friend," said the Djinn, "what's this I hear of your doing no work, with the world so new-and-all?"

"Humph!" said the Camel.

The Djinn sat down, with his chin in his hand, and began to think a Great Magic, while the Camel looked at his own reflection in the pool of water.

"You've given the Three extra work ever since Monday morning, all on account of your 'scruciating idleness," said the Djinn; and he went on thinking Magics, with his chin in his hand.

"Humph!" said the Camel.

"I shouldn't say that again if I were you," said the Djinn.

And the Camel said, "Humph!" again; but no sooner had he said it than he saw his back, that he was so proud of, puffing up and puffing up into a great big lolloping humph.

"Do you see that?" said the Djinn. "That's your very own humph that you've brought upon your very own self by not working. Today is Thursday, and you've done no work since Monday, when the work began. Now you are going to work."

"How can I," said the Camel, "with this humph on my back?"

That's made a-purpose," said the Djinn, "all because you missed those three days. You will be able to work now for three days without eating, because you can live on your humph."

And the Camel humphed himself, humph and all, and went away to join the Three. And from that day to this the Camel always wears a humph (we call it "hump" now, not to hurt his feelings).

From *Just So Stories*

Dr. Dolittle's Pushmi-Pullyu

By Hugh Lofting

DR. DOLITTLE loved animals so much that he decided, instead of doctoring people, he would be an animal doctor. On the advice of Chee-Chee, his pet monkey, he made the long voyage to Africa to cure the monkeys there of a strange disease. That done, he told the monkeys that he must go back to his home in Puddleby.

They were very surprised at this; for they had thought that he was going to stay with them forever. And that night all the monkeys got together in the jungle to talk it over.

And the Chief Chimpanzee rose up and said, "Why is it the good man is going away? Is he not happy here with us?"

But none of them could answer him.

Then the Grand Gorilla got up and said, "I think we all should go to him and ask him to stay. Perhaps if we make him a new house and a bigger bed, and promise him plenty of monkey-servants to work for him and to make life pleasant for him—perhaps then he will not wish to go."

Then Chee-Chee got up; and all the others whispered, "Sh! Look! Chee-Chee, the great Traveler, is about to speak!"

And Chee-Chee said to the other monkeys, "My friends, I am afraid it is useless to ask the Doctor to stay. He owes money in Puddleby; and he says he must go back and pay it."

And the monkeys asked him, "What is *money?"*

Then Chee-Chee told them that in the Land of the White Men you could get nothing without money—that it was almost impossible to *live* without money.

And some of them asked, "But can you not even eat and drink without paying?"

Chee-Chee shook his head. And then he told them that even he, when he was with the organ-grinder, had been made to ask the children for money.

And the Chief Chimpanzee turned to the Oldest Orang-outang and said, "Cousin, surely these Men be strange creatures! Who would wish to live in such a land? My gracious, how paltry!"

Then Chee-Chee said, "When we were coming to you we had no boat to cross the sea in and no money to buy food to eat on our journey. So a man lent us some biscuits; and we said we would pay him when we came back. And we borrowed a boat from a sailor; but it was broken on the rocks when we reached the shores of Africa. Now the Doctor says he must go back and get the sailor another boat—because the man was poor and his ship was all he had."

And the monkeys were all silent for a while, sitting quite still upon the ground and thinking hard.

At last the Biggest Baboon got up and said, "I do not think we ought to let this good man leave our land till we have given him a fine present to take with him, so that he may know we are grateful for all that he has done for us."

And a little, tiny red monkey who was sitting up in a tree shouted down, "I think that, too!"

And then they all cried out, making a great noise, "Yes, yes. Let us give him the finest present a White Man ever had!"

Now they began to wonder and ask one another what would be the best thing to give him. And one said, "Fifty bags of coconuts!" And another, "A hundred bunches of bananas! At least he shall not have to buy his fruit in the Land Where You Pay to Eat!"

But Chee-Chee told them that all these things would be too heavy to carry so far and would go bad before half of them were eaten.

"If you want to please him," he said, "give him an animal. You may be sure he will be kind to it. Give him some rare animal they have not got in the menageries."

And the monkeys asked him, "What are *menageries?*"

Then Chee-Chee explained to them that menageries were places in the Land of the White Men, where animals were put in cages for people to come and look at. And the monkeys were very shocked and said to one another,

"These Men are like thoughtless young ones—stupid and easily amused. Sh! It is a prison he means."

So then they asked Chee-Chee what rare animal it could be that they should give the Doctor—one the White Men had not seen before. And the Major of the Marmosettes asked,

"Have they an iguana over there?"

But Chee-Chee said, "Yes, there is one in the London Zoo."

And another asked, "Have they an okapi?"

But Chee-Chee said, "Yes. In Belgium where my organ-grinder took me five years ago, they had an okapi in a big city they call Antwerp."

And another asked, "Have they a pushmi-pullyu?"

Then Chee-Chee said, "No. No White Man has ever seen a pushmi-pullyu. Let us give him that."

Pushmi-pullyus are now extinct. That means, there aren't any more. But long ago, when Doctor Dolittle was alive, there were some of them still left in the deepest jungles of Africa; and even then they were very scarce. They had no tail, but a head at each end, and sharp horns on each head. They were very shy and terribly hard to catch. The black men get most of their animals by sneaking up behind them. But you could not do this with the pushmi-pullyu—because, no matter which way you came towards him, he was always facing you. And besides, only one half of him slept at a time. The other head was always awake—and watching. This was why they were never caught and never seen in zoos. Though many of the greatest huntsmen and the cleverest menagerie-keepers spent years of their lives searching through the jungles in all weathers for pushmi-pullyus, not a single one had ever been caught.

Well, the monkeys set out hunting for this animal through the forest. And after they had gone a good many miles, one of them found peculiar footprints near the edge of a river; and they knew that a pushmi-pullyu must be near that spot.

Then they went along the bank of the river a little way and they saw a place where the grass was high and thick; and they guessed that he was in there.

So they all joined hands and made a great circle round the high grass. The pushmi-pullyu heard them coming; and he tried hard to break through the ring of monkeys. But he couldn't do it. When he saw that it was no use trying to escape, he sat down and waited to see what they wanted.

They asked him if he would go with Doctor Dolittle and be put on show in the Land of the White Men.

But he shook both his heads hard and said, "Certainly not!"

They explained to him that he would not be shut up in a menagerie but would just be looked at. They told him that the Doctor was a very kind man but hadn't any money; and people would pay to see a two-headed animal and the Doctor would get rich and could pay for the boat he had borrowed to come to Africa in.

But he answered, "No. You know how shy I am—I hate being stared at." And he almost began to cry.

Then for three days they tried to persuade him.

And at the end of the third day he said he would come with them and see what kind of a man the Doctor was, first.

So the monkeys traveled back with the pushmi-pullyu. And when they came to where the Doctor's little house of grass was, they knocked on the door.

The duck, who was packing the trunk, said, "Come in!"

And Chee-Chee very proudly took the animal inside and

showed him to the Doctor.

"What in the world is it?" asked John Dolittle, gazing at the strange creature.

"Lord save us!" cried the duck. "How does it make up its mind?"

"It doesn't look to me as though it had any," said Jip, the dog.

"This, Doctor," said Chee-Chee, "is the pushmi-pullyu—the rarest animal of the African jungles, the only two-headed beast in the world! Take him home with you and your fortune's made. People will pay any money to see him."

"But I don't want any money," said the Doctor.

"Yes, you do," said Dab-Dab, the duck. "Don't you remember how we had to pinch and scrape to pay the butcher's bill in Puddleby? And how are you going to get the sailor the new boat you spoke of—unless we have money?"

"I was going to make him one," said the Doctor.

"Oh, do be sensible!" cried Dab-Dab. "Where would you get all the wood and the nails to make one with? And besides, what are we going to live on? We shall be poorer than ever when we get back. Chee-Chee's perfectly right; take the funny-looking thing along, do!"

"Well, perhaps there is something in what you say," murmured the Doctor. "It certainly would make a new kind of pet. But does the er—what-do-you-call-it really want to go?"

"Yes, I'll go," said the pushmi-pullyu who saw at once, from the Doctor's face, that he was a man to be trusted. "You have been so kind to the animals here—and the monkeys tell me that I am the only one who will do. But you must promise me that if

I do not like it in the Land of the White Men you will send me back."

"Why certainly—of course," said the Doctor. "Excuse me, surely you are related to the Deer Family, are you not?"

"Yes," said the pushmi-pullyu, "to the Abyssinian Gazelles and the Asiatic Chamois—on my mother's side. My father's great-grandfather was the last of the Unicorns."

"Most interesting!" murmured the Doctor; and he took a book out of the trunk which Dab-Dab was packing and began turning the pages. "Let us see if Buffon says anything—"

"I notice," said the duck, "that you only talk with one of your mouths. Can't the other head talk as well?"

"Oh, yes," said the pushmi-pullyu. "But I keep the other mouth for eating—mostly. In that way I can talk while I am eating without being rude. Our people have always been very polite."

When the packing was finished and everything was ready to start, the monkeys gave a grand party for the Doctor, and all the animals of the jungle came. And they had pineapples and mangoes and honey and all sorts of good things to eat and drink.

After they had all finished eating, the Doctor got up and said, "My friends: I am not clever at speaking long words after dinner, like some men; and I have just eaten many fruits and much honey. But I wish to tell you that I am very sad at leaving your beautiful country. Because I have things to do in the Land of the White Men, I must go. After I have gone, remember never to let the flies settle on your food before you eat it; and do not sleep on the ground when the rains are coming. I—er—er—I hope you will all live happily ever after."

When the Doctor stopped speaking and sat down, all the monkeys clapped their hands a long time and said to one another, "Let it be remembered always among our people that he sat and ate with us, here, under the trees. For surely he is the Greatest of Men!"

And the Grand Gorilla, who had the strength of seven horses in his hairy arms, rolled a great rock up to the head of the table and said,

"This stone for all time shall mark the spot."

And even to this day, in the heart of the jungle, that stone still is there. And monkey-mothers, passing through the forest with their families, still point down at it from the branches and whisper to their children, "Sh! There it is—look—where the Good White Man sat and ate food with us in the Year of the Great Sickness!"

Then, when the party was over, the Doctor and his pets started out to go back to the seashore. And all the monkeys went with him as far as the edge of their country, carrying his trunk and bags, to see him off.

From *The Story of Doctor Dolittle*

The Last of the Dragons

By E. Nesbit

OF COURSE you know that dragons were once as common as motorbuses are now, and almost as dangerous. But as every well-brought-up prince was expected to kill a dragon and rescue a princess, the dragons grew fewer and fewer. And at last there were no more dragons in France and no more dragons in Germany, or Spain, or Italy, or Russia. There were some left in China, and are still, but they are cold and bronzy, and there never were any, of course, in America. But the last real live dragon left was in England, and of course that was a very long time ago, before what you call "English History" began. This dragon lived in Cornwall in the big caves amidst the rocks, and was a very fine big dragon, quite seventy feet long from the tip of its fearful snout to the end of its terrible tail. It breathed fire and smoke, and rattled when it walked, because its scales were made of iron. Its wings were like half-umbrellas—or like bat's wings, only several thousand times bigger.

Now the King of Cornwall had one daughter, and when she was sixteen, of course, she would have to go and face

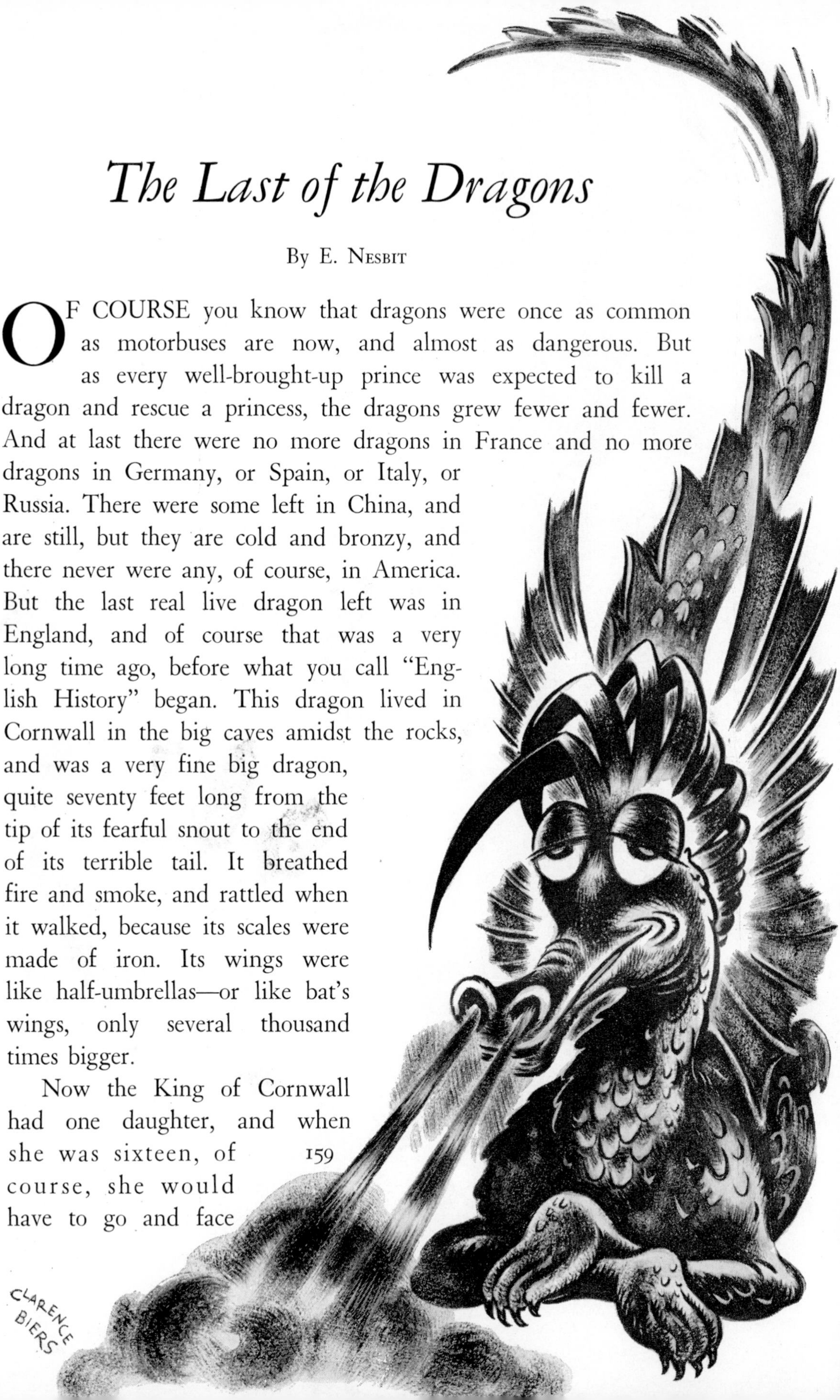

CLARENCE BIERS

the dragon. Such tales are always told in royal nurseries at twilight, so the Princess knew what she had to expect. The dragon would not eat her, of course—because the prince would come and rescue her. But the Princess could not help thinking it would be much pleasanter to have nothing to do with the dragon at all—not even to be rescued from him.

"All the princes I know are such very silly little boys," she told her father. "Why must I be rescued by a prince?"

"It's always done, my dear," said the King, taking his crown off and putting it on the grass, for they were alone in the garden, and even kings must unbend sometimes.

"Father, darling," said the Princess presently, when she had made a daisy chain and put it on the king's head, where the crown ought to have been, "couldn't we tie up one of the silly little princes for the dragon to look at—and then I could go and kill the dragon and rescue the Prince? I fence much better than any of the princes we know."

"What an unladylike idea!" said the King, and put his crown on again, for he saw the Prime Minister coming with a basket of newlaid Bills for him to sign. "Dismiss the thought, my child. I rescued your mother from a dragon, and you don't want to set yourself up above her, I should hope?"

"But this is the *last* dragon. It is different from all other dragons."

"How?" asked the King.

"Because he *is* the last," said the Princess, and went off to her fencing lesson, with which she took great pains. She took great pains with all her lessons—for she could not give up the idea of fighting the dragon. She took such pains that she became the strongest and boldest and most skillful and most sensible princess in Europe.

And the days and years went on, till at last the day came which was the day before the Princess was to be rescued from the dragon. The prince who was to do this deed of valor was a pale prince, with large eyes and a head full of mathematics and philosophy, but he had unfortunately neglected his fencing lessons. He was to stay the night at the palace, and there was a banquet.

After supper the Princess sent her pet parrot to the Prince with a note. It said: "Please, Prince, come onto the terrace. I want to talk to you without anybody else hearing.—The Princess."

So, of course, he went. And when he came quite close to her, he said, "Princess, at your service," and bent his cloth-of-gold-covered knee and put his hand on his cloth-of-gold-covered heart.

"Do you think," said the Princess earnestly, "that you will be able to kill the dragon?"

"I will kill the dragon," said the Prince firmly, "or perish in the attempt."

"It's no use your perishing," said the Princess.

"It's the least I can do," said the Prince.

"What I'm afraid of is that it'll be the most you can do," said the Princess.

"It's the only thing I can do," said he, "unless I kill the dragon."

"Why you should do anything for me is what I can't see," said she.

"But I want to," he said. "You must know that I love you better than anything in the world."

When he said that, he looked so kind that the Princess began to like him a little.

"Look here," she said. "You know they tie me to a rock, and leave me—and then everybody scurries home and puts up the shutters and keeps them shut till you ride through the town shouting that you've killed the dragon, and I ride on the horse behind you weeping for joy."

"I've heard that that is how it is done," said he.

"Well, do you love me well enough to come very quickly and set me free—and we'll fight the dragon together?"

"It wouldn't be safe for you."

"Much safer for both of us for me to be free, with a sword in my hand, then tied up and helpless. *Do* agree."

He could refuse her nothing. So he agreed. And next day everything happened as she had said.

When he had cut the cords that tied her to the rocks they stood on the lonely mountainside looking at each other.

"It seems to me," said the Prince, "that this ceremony could have been arranged without the dragon."

"Yes," said the Princess, "but since it has been arranged with the dragon—"

"It seems such a pity to kill the dragon—the last in the world," said the Prince.

"Well, then, don't let's," said the Princess. "Let's tame it not to eat princesses but to eat out of their hands. They say everything can be tamed by kindness."

"Taming by kindness means giving them things to eat," said the Prince. "Have you got anything to eat?"

She hadn't, but the Prince owned that he had a few biscuits. "Breakfast was so very early," said he, "and I thought you might have felt faint after the fight."

"How clever," said the Princess, and they took a biscuit in each hand. And they looked here and they looked there, but never a dragon could they see.

"But here's its trail," said the Prince, and pointed to where the rock was scarred and scratched so as to make a track leading to the mouth of a dark cave. It was like cart ruts in a Sussex road, mixed with the marks of sea gulls' feet on the sea sand. "Look, that's where it's dragged its brass tail and planted its steel claws."

"Don't let's think how hard its tail and its claws are," said the Princess, "or I shall begin to be frightened. And I know you can't tame anything, even by kindness, if you're frightened of it. Come on. Now or never."

She caught the Prince's hand in hers and they ran along the path towards the dark mouth of the cave. But they did not run into it. It really was so very *dark*.

So they stood outside, and the Prince shouted, "What ho! Dragon there! What ho within!" And from the cave they heard an answering voice, and great clattering and creaking. It sounded as though a rather large cotton mill were stretching itself and waking up out of its sleep.

The Prince and the Princess trembled, but they stood firm.

"Dragon—I say, Dragon!" said the Princess, "do come out and talk to us. We've brought you a present."

"Oh, yes—I know your presents," growled the dragon in a

huge rumbling voice. "One of those precious princesses, I suppose? And I've got to come out and fight for her. Well, I tell you straight, I'm not going to do it. A fair fight I wouldn't say no to—a fair fight and no favor—but one of these put-up fights where you've got to lose—no. So I tell you. If I wanted a princess I'd come and take her, but I don't. What do you suppose I'd do with her, if I'd got her?"

"Eat her, wouldn't you?" said the Princess in a voice that trembled a little.

"Eat a fiddlestick end," said the dragon very rudely. "I wouldn't touch the horrid thing."

The Princess's voice grew firmer.

"Do you like biscuits?" she asked.

"No," growled the Dragon.

"Not the nice little expensive ones with sugar on the top?"

"*No*," growled the dragon.

"Then what *do* you like?" asked the Prince.

"You go away and don't bother me," growled the dragon. They could hear it turn over, and the clang and clatter of its turning echoed in the cave like the sound of steam hammers.

The Prince and the Princess looked at each other. What *were* they to do? It was no use going home and telling the King that the dragon didn't want princesses. His Majesty was old-fashioned and would never believe that a new-fashioned dragon could be different from an old-fashioned dragon. They could not go into the cave and kill the dragon. Indeed, unless he attacked the Princess it did not seem fair to kill him at all.

"He must like something," whispered the Princess, and she called out in a voice as sweet as honey and sugar cane:

"Dragon! Dragon, dear!"

"WHAT?" shouted the dragon. "Say that again!" They could hear the dragon coming towards them through the darkness. The Princess shivered, and said in a very small voice:

"Dragon—dragon, dear!"

And then the dragon came out. The Prince drew his sword and the Princess drew hers—the beautiful silver-handled one that the Prince had brought in his motor car. But they did not attack; they moved slowly back as the dragon came out, all the vast scaly length of him, and lay along the rock—his great wings half spread and his silvery sheen gleaming like diamonds in the sun. At last they could retreat no farther—the dark rock behind them stopped their way. With their backs to the rock they stood, swords in hand, and waited.

The dragon drew nearer and nearer—and now they could see that he was not breathing fire and smoke as they had expected. He came crawling slowly towards them, wriggling a little as a puppy does when it wants to play and isn't quite sure whether or not you're cross with it.

And then they saw that great tears were coursing down its brazen cheeks.

"Whatever's the matter?" asked the Prince.

CLARENCE
BIERS

"Nobody," sobbed the dragon, "ever called me 'dear' before!"

"Don't cry, dragon dear," said the Princess. "We'll call you 'dear' as often as you like. We want to tame you."

"I *am* tame," said the dragon, "that's just it. That's what nobody but you has ever found out. I'm so tame that I'd eat out of your hands."

"Eat what, dragon dear?" said the Princess. "Not biscuits?"

The dragon slowly shook its heavy head.

"Not biscuits?" said the Princess tenderly. "What, then, dragon dear?"

"Your kindness quite undragons me," it said. "No one has ever asked any of us what we like to eat—always offering us princesses, and then rescuing them—and never once, 'What'll you take to drink the King's health in?' Cruel hard I call it," and it wept again.

"But what would you like to drink our health in?" said the Prince. "We're going to be married, aren't we, Princess?"

She said that she supposed so.

"What'll I take to drink your health in?" asked the dragon. "Ah, you're a gentleman, sir. I'll be proud to drink your and your lady's health in a tiddy drop of"—its voice faltered—"to think of you asking me so friendly like," it said. "Yes, sir, just a tiddy drop of puppuppuppuppupetrol (gasoline)—tha—that's what does a dragon good, sir——"

"I've lots in the car," said the Prince, and was off down the mountain. He was a good judge of character, and he knew that with this dragon the Princess would be safe.

"If I might make so bold," said the dragon, "while the gentleman's away—p'raps just to pass the time you'd be so kind as to call me 'Dear' again, and if you'd shake claws with a poor old dragon that's never been anybody's enemy but his own—well, the last of the dragons'll be the proudest dragon there's ever been since the first of them."

It held out an enormous paw, and the great steel hooks that were its claws closed over the Princess's hand as softly as the claws of the Himalayan bear will close over the bun you hand it through the bars at the Zoo.

And so the Prince and Princess went back to the palace, the dragon following them like a pet dog. And all through the wedding festivities no one drank more earnestly to the happiness of the bride and

bridegroom than the Princess's pet dragon, whom she at once named Fido.

When the happy pair were settled in their own kingdom, Fido came to them and begged to be allowed to make himself useful.

"There must be some little thing I can do," he said, rattling his wings and stretching his claws. "My wings and claws and so on ought to be turned to some account—to say nothing of my grateful heart."

So the Prince had a special saddle or howdah made for him—like the tops of many tramcars fitted together. One hundred and fifty seats were fitted to this, and the dragon, whose greatest pleasure was now to give pleasure to others, delighted in taking parties of children to the seaside. It flew through the air with its

hundred and fifty little passengers, and would lie on the sand patiently waiting till they were ready to return. The children were very fond of it and used to call it "Dear," a word which never failed to bring tears to its eyes. So it lived, useful and respected, till some one happened to say, in his hearing, that dragons were out of date, now so much new machinery had come. This so distressed him that he asked the King to change him into something less old-fashioned, and the kindly monarch at once changed him into a mechanical contrivance. The dragon, indeed, became the first airplane.

From *Five of Us—and Madeline*

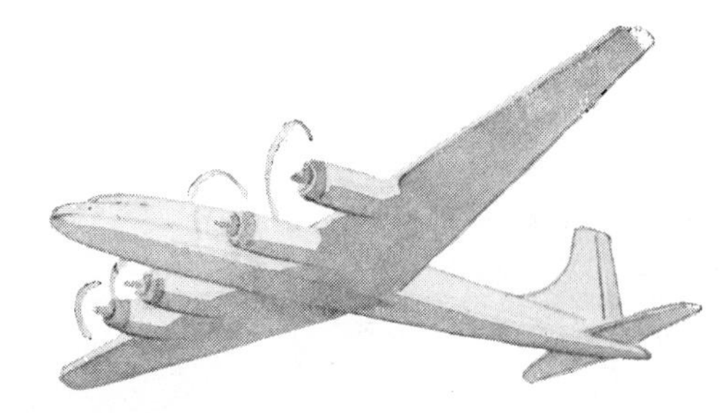

WHEELS, WINGS, AND REAL THINGS

The Little Old Truck

BY J. MORRIS JONES

THE LITTLE red truck whizzed along the highway at a merry clip. Around and around went its wheels, faster and faster. Never before had it started on such a happy journey. Even the engine was humming a cheerful song.

"Beep, beep! Beep, beep!" sang the truck's horn. "This is the day before Christmas, and I am on my way to Pine Tree Hollow with the most exciting load I have ever carried."

Only that morning when it was parked by the loading platform at the department store, the truck had heard one of the men saying, "Someone forgot to send these Christmas packages to the boys and girls at Pine Tree Hollow. We can't send them by train for the railroad doesn't go there. We can't send them by airplane for there is no airport at the little town. And we can't use any of our delivery trucks. They are much too busy. Pine Tree Hollow isn't even on a highway. It is away off there by itself back of nowhere. There is only one thing left for us to do. This little truck must take the load. Unless it gets a flat tire, it will surely get to Pine Tree Hollow in time."

You can imagine how proud the little truck felt as it started on its long trip. And no wonder, for its load of gifts was enough to dazzle anyone with its gaily colored wrapping paper and ribbons. There were red, blue, and yellow packages. There were violet, orange, and green ones. And there were still more in wrappings with as many different shades of color as you would find in a paint factory.

Inside the packages, carefully hidden, were dolls, dishes, and toy animals of every kind, shape, and color. There were footballs, baseballs, airplanes, automobiles, knives, cowboy suits, and colored marbles. Better still there were candies, chewing gum, and cookies. It was, indeed, a load of gifts which would gladden the heart of every boy and girl in Pine Tree Hollow.

But it wasn't long before the sun went behind a cloud, and the wind began to blow. Then the truck saw something that made its engine go even faster than before. It was a big, fat snowflake. Then another fell, and another, and another. Before you could say "Pine Tree Hollow," it was snowing heavily, and the headlights could hardly see a thing in front of them.

As the snow got thicker, the little truck had to slow down. But when it saw a steep hill ahead, the engine almost stopped from fright. The only way it could hope to get up that hill was to make a run for it and hope for the best. The truck had barely begun its uphill climb when the wheels began to go around and around with a whining snarl. They were going around even faster than before. But the truck was not going up the hill. It just stayed in the same place as the wheels went around and around.

"Oh dear," thought the little truck.

"What shall I do now? What shall I do? I must get these packages to the boys and girls of Pine Tree Hollow today. I must, I must, I must. They are counting on me."

Just then, a big cross-country bus came down the road. "Beep, beep!" honked the little truck. "Please help me up the hill with my load of toys. I must get to Pine Tree Hollow today."

But the big bus did not stop. It just sent the snow flying and said, "Out of my way! Out of my way! I am taking a lot of people home for Christmas. I can't be bothered with a piece of old junk like you."

So the bus scattered the snow far and wide as it roared around the truck with its exhaust pipe blowing out a cloud of jet-black smoke. And on up the hill it went, leaving two broad wheel tracks in the white snow.

A little while later, a huge trailer truck came lumbering along. "Beep, beep!" went the truck's horn. "Beep, beep! Please help me up the hill with my load of toys. I must get to Pine Tree Hollow today. I must, I must, I must."

The big truck was carrying a full load. It could not carry another single package, but it stopped. "I would like to help you," it said, "and I would be glad to pull you up the hill if I only had a rope or chain. But I don't, so I must go on and deliver this load." And on up the hill went the trailer truck, in the wheel tracks which the bus had made in the snow.

THE LITTLE OLD TRUCK

Just as it went over the top of the hill, a brand new automobile came proudly through the snow. "Beep, beep! Please help me up the hill with my load of toys. Please help me," said the little truck. But the new automobile just looked down its radiator at the little truck with its load of Christmas gifts. And on up the hill it went, along the two tracks left in the snow by the bus and truck.

As the automobile disappeared, the truck heard something else. It went, "Clickety, clickety, clickety, clack! Clickety, clickety, clickety, clack!" It was a train chugging down the railroad track which ran parallel to the road. As it came near, the big engine saw the little truck and snorted—

Puff—fuff—fuff—fuff!
You—can't—do—it.
Puff—fuff—fuff—fuff!
You—can't—do—it.

The engine blew a shrill note on its whistle and it sent out a huge cloud of steam and smoke

as it entered the tunnel under the hill with a—

Puff—fuff—fuff—fuff!
You—can't—do—it.
Puff—fuff—fuff—fuff!
You—can't—do—it.

"Of all things," said the truck angrily. "What a snooty old engine! I wish I could push its Puff—fuff—fuff—fuff down its chimney." At that moment, a farm boy came running up to the little truck. He was bringing a pair of rusty chains.

In no time at all, he had the chains hooked on the rear wheels. This time, when the truck tried to go on, the wheels took hold. They did not just turn around and around and around with a whining snarl.

"Beep, beep!" honked the truck. "Many thanks!" And on up the hill it went in the two tracks left in the snow.

On the other side of the hill, the train was coming out of the tunnel. And the big engine was still saying—

Puff—fuff—fuff—fuff!
You—can't—do—it.
Puff—fuff—fuff—fuff!
You—can't—do—it.

But it could not see the little truck now, and it could not hear the rusty old chains clank against the fenders as it went slowly but surely up the hill with a—

Clink—clank—clank—clank!
I—CAN—do—it.
Clink—clank—clank—clank!
I—CAN—do—it.

THE LITTLE OLD TRUCK

And the little truck did do it, for it finally reached the top of the hill. There in the distance far below was the branch road leading from the highway to Pine Tree Hollow. In going down hill, the chains went faster and faster with their

Clink—clank—clank—clank!
I—KNEW—I—could.
Clink—clank—clank—clank!
I—KNEW—I—could.

It caught up with the big engine which had changed its tune to—

Puff—fuff—fuff—fuff!
You—said—you—could.
Puff—fuff—fuff—fuff!
You—said—you—could.

And all the way to Pine Tree Hollow, the chains sang their merry tune against the fenders—

Clink—clank—clank—clank!
Of—course—I—could.
Clink—clank—clank—clank!
Of—course—I—could.

The Family Who Had Never Had Roller Skates

By Hildegard Woodward

IT WAS springtime in the city. The hand organs were playing the Bella Bocca Polka and everyone was roller skating. People whirled gaily along the sidewalks and through the park. Sometimes they fell on their elbows and often their feet flew up in the air.

This was quite long ago, that is, long before anyone knew about automobiles, for time was when the park was full of horses and carriages and some people scorched along on high-wheeled bicycles. But roller skating was new and quite the thing. Yet, sad as it may seem, Emma, Alice, and Louise Pettingill had never had roller skates.

"You would break your legs," said Pa-pa Pettingill.

"Dear me, yes," said Ma-ma Pettingill.

"Little ladies should not muss and tear their petticoats," said Cousin Margaret Pettingill.

THE FAMILY WHO HAD NEVER HAD ROLLER SKATES

So Emma, Alice, and Louise Pettingill just stood at the parlor window and gazed at the people skimming along through the park. They wished their legs were not so brittle nor their petticoats so stiff. They were quiet, good little girls who always did what they were told and never asked for anything they couldn't have. Dreams of roller skates rolled through their heads but they said nothing. They just sighed sadly and stood at the parlor window in their stiff petticoats, quietly humming the Bella Bocca Polka.

When Cousin Margaret Pettingill took them for their walk in the park she never seemed to notice that everyone was roller skating; boys and girls, papas and mamas, cousins and uncles, even aunts. Everyone was roller skating; that is, everyone except Emma, Alice, and Louise Pettingill. When they went downtown shopping she didn't even seem to notice that the window of the Empire Emporium was just full of roller skates, beautiful, gleaming roller skates of all sizes. Emma,

HILDEGARD WOODWARD

Alice, and Louise gazed longingly at them but it did no good. Cousin Margaret Pettingill walked right ahead, bent on buying yards of ribbon for more sashes, and yards and yards of lace for petticoat frills.

"Why don't you roller-skate?" called Polly Polhemus as she whirled around them on one foot. "See what fun it is."

Emma, Alice, and Louise had nothing whatever to say. They just plodded along home in their button boots, looking very prim and proper but feeling quite unhappy.

"What nice ladylike girls we have," said Cousin Margaret Pettingill. "I am so glad they do not care to indulge in boisterous performances on roller skates."

"Yes, indeed," said Ma-ma Pettingill.

The three little girls grew sadder and quieter day by day. They didn't even care to eat. Their legs grew thinner and their cheeks grew paler, but the Pettingill petticoats were always clean and freshly starched and never torn.

Pa-pa Pettingill was far too busy at business to notice their plight. He dashed out of the house every morning after breakfast and when he slowly climbed the brown front steps at night, he never even looked up from his evening paper.

One day, however, something happened. Pa-pa Pettingill forgot to get an evening paper. So when he came down the street to his house he did notice Emma, Alice, and Louise stand-

ing at the parlor window gazing out at the park. They looked so thin and sad that he suddenly darted for the front steps and ran right into a sailor who was swirling along the sidewalk on his roller skates. This did not particularly please Pa-pa Pettingill, and he flew up the brownstone steps in quite a state and started shouting in the front hall at Ma-ma Pettingill.

"What is the meaning of this! Our daughters look ill. We must get tonics and pills and medicines. They must be cured at once!"

"Yes, my dear," said Ma-ma Pettingill. "I'll send Peter for Doctor Martin tomorrow."

"Send for him immediately," roared Pa-pa Pettingill.

Emma, Alice, and Louise became frightened and paler than ever, but they didn't say anything at all. The whole family waited in the parlor while Peter Onderdouck, the coachman, hitched the horse and drove around to tell Doctor Martin.

Finally, after an hour or two, Doctor Martin came, medicine bag in hand.

"Thank you for coming so promptly," said Ma-ma Pettingill.

Emma, Alice, and Louise began to tremble while Doctor Martin listened to their hearts and took their temperatures. He looked at their tongues and examined their throats. Then, hum-

ming the Bella Bocca Polka, he threw his things in his bag.

"Pills! Tonics! Nonsense!" he cried.

"Perhaps they should be put to bed with flannel on their chests and keep out the air," said Cousin Margaret Pettingill.

"Yes," said Ma-ma Pettingill, "the spring air is so dangerous."

"Nonsense," roared Doctor Martin, "they must have fresh air and plenty of it. Flannel, indeed! Get out their roller skates and send them to the park."

"But we have no roller skates," murmured Emma, Alice, and Louise Pettingill.

"What, no roller skates!" he shouted. "I am astounded!"

"Oh!" said Pa-pa and Ma-ma Pettingill.

"So very unladylike," murmured Cousin Margaret Pettingill.

"Ridiculous!" said Doctor Martin. "Everyone is roller-skating. Send out for some at once."

THE FAMILY WHO HAD NEVER HAD ROLLER SKATES

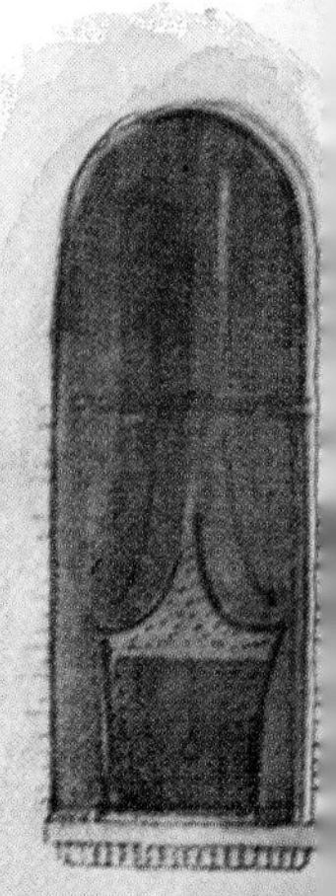

The next day Peter Onderdouck hitched up and drove Pa-pa Pettingill around to the Empire Emporium where he himself bought three pairs of the shiniest, most wonderful roller skates with wooden wheels that whirled like anything.

So Emma, Alice, and Louise began to roller-skate. They fell on their noses, their feet flew up in the air. Their petticoats grew mussed and torn, but their cheeks grew rosy. Soon there were no finer roller skaters than Emma, Alice, and Louise Pettingill.

Then Pa-pa and Ma-ma and Cousin Margaret Pettingill stood proudly watching from the parlor window.

"I have half a mind to try it myself," said Pa-pa Pettingill.

"Dear me," said Ma-ma Pettingill.

"What next!" exclaimed Cousin Margaret Pettingill, but, very softly, she began to hum the Bella Bocca Polka.

From *Time Was*

Timmy Rides the China Clipper

By Carol Nay

ON A Wednesday afternoon in mid-December, a young boy stood on Treasure Island in San Francisco Bay. His eyes glistened with excitement as he watched men load the Clipper Ship that lay anchored in the Lagoon. Soon these great wings spreading before him would be carrying a cargo of men and mail across the sea to China. And he, Timmy Blake, would be a part of that cargo!

He was going to spend Christmas with his Aunt Kate and

Uncle George in far-off Hong Kong. Far-off, indeed! Did it not take ocean liners weeks to reach the Orient? Yet, in this Clipper Ship, China lay west only six days away.

So lost was Timmy in his thoughts that he scarcely felt a man tap his shoulder and say, "Timmy Blake? This way, please. We have to weigh you before you go aboard."

Timmy followed and stepped up on the scales. Eagerly he turned toward his father and mother who now stood beside him. "I weigh ninety pounds, Dad," he said bravely. "It won't be long 'til I'll be as heavy as you."

"Still, you are the lightest passenger on the Clipper Ship," replied his father. "How does this sound: ninety pounds of boy with seventy-seven pounds of baggage bound for China on a forty-one-and-one-half-ton plane?"

"Like the chance of a lifetime," murmured Timmy's mother. "Few boys have an aunt and uncle to send them a ticket to fly to China. We're going to miss you, Timmy, but I know you are going to have the most wonderful trip."

Now the crew began to assemble, and suddenly a bell echoed loudly through the terminal. There was a great stir among the passengers, who looked with eager faces through the door. Presently the Captain and his crew of eleven filed down the landing to board the waiting ship. A moment later the great bird began to tremble with life as the roar of its four motors pierced the stillness.

Then the bell rang twice, and the terminal door opened for the passengers to file down to the ship. Timmy's heart began to pound with excitement. He kissed his mother and father good-by and hurried down the landing. What a never-to-be-forgotten thrill he felt as he stepped briskly onto the float and waited his turn to cross the gangplank!

And how small he seemed, standing there before that enormous streamlined plane! How gigantic it loomed, poised and ready

for its long flight! His blue eyes widened as his gaze followed the spread of the great wings from tip to tip, a distance of one hundred and fifty-two feet.

Upon entering the hull, Timmy descended three steps into a large dining room and recreation center. From there a steward led him to a compartment and bade him to be seated.

"We fasten your safety belt for all take-offs and landings," he explained, as he deftly adjusted the straps. "Merely a regulation. No danger."

As other passengers entered his compartment, Timmy was too occupied to heed them. Through the windows he stared at the crowd behind the wire fence of the terminal yard. Dimly he could see his parents in the foreground and he waved gaily, hoping that they could see him.

Somewhere near a clock struck four, and immediately the ship began to move slowly from the landing and head up the bay. For forty-five seconds it skimmed the waves as it gained speed. Then, with a terrific roar, it shook off the clutch of the sea and rose gracefully into the air.

Up! Up! it soared, until the Golden Gate and the brown California hills resembled a relief map in the background. Soon the coast line was lost to view in a new world that was strangely beautiful to behold; a world of rippling sea and misty sky as far as his wondering eyes could reach.

At last he turned from the window and began to study his surroundings. There were ten passengers in his compartment. On the starboard side, his companions were seated on a pair of triple seats which faced each other. On the port side, there were double seats in the same position. The upholstering was a soft tan wool with leather trimmings that contrasted pleasantly with the green carpet and lighter green walls.

Presently a steward in a smart blue uniform approached Timmy. "Well, young man, are you enjoying your trip?"

"You bet I am!" cried Timmy enthusiastically. "How high are we flying right now, sir?"

"About eight thousand feet. And we're cruising along at one hundred and fifty miles an hour."

"Wow!" cried Timmy in amazement. "Are we going that fast?"

"Yes, that's about average speed," laughed the steward, "but it will get us to Honolulu by tomorrow morning." He paused, then added, "I am Mr. Barton, the Flight Steward. Suppose I show you through the ship now, so that you'll be familiar with your home for the next few days."

The boy rose quickly, and followed Mr. Barton to the rear of the ship. Here they entered a most attractive deluxe compartment with bright-blue upholstered furnishings, a built-in love seat, odd tables, and a large easy chair. A prominent actor and his wife occupied the rooms now, and they invited the sightseers to visit them again.

Mr. Barton then proceeded to lead the way through a series of compartments, like the one in which Timmy was traveling. "There are five of these large compartments," he said, "and a sixth, which seats only four persons, in addition to the large dining room that you saw when you came aboard. The seats are converted into upper and lower berths on our night flight to Honolulu. Then we can sleep as many as thirty-four passengers. During the rest of the trip, however, we could carry as many as seventy-four on our list, besides the crew."

Mr. Barton went on to explain that after they left Honolulu, the hops to Midway, Wake, Guam, Manila, and China were flown during the day. "Of course, we spend the afternoon and night on shore at each stop to rest and refuel," he said. "We carry also a valuable cargo of mail and air express which we leave at these ports."

Now Mr. Barton and Timmy approached the main lounge and recreation room, which served also as a dining salon when tables were placed between chairs for the meal service.

"I smell something good," said Timmy, as the Flight Steward opened the door and led the way into a spotless kitchen. "This is the galley where my assistant and I prepare the meals and refreshments. We'll soon serve you a full-course dinner, and plenty of ice cream just for you."

Timmy stared about the galley. "But how are you going to cook everything?" he asked, puzzled.

"Dinner is brought aboard already cooked," answered the Flight Steward. "All we do is to heat it up and help serve it. The food is kept warm in that cabinet by hot air discharged from one of the motors."

"What about breakfast?" asked Timmy eagerly.

Mr. Barton laughed at this. "You may have two breakfasts, Timmy, if you can hold them. One aboard the plane, and, if you wish, a later one at the Royal Hawaiian Hotel in Honolulu."

Suddenly Timmy Blake began to realize what a great distance they were spanning so easily on this overnight flight to Hawaii. Why, tomorrow when the sun rose, he would be 2,400 miles away from his California home.

"Just what would happen if our motors should stop on us right now?" asked Timmy, suddenly.

Mr. Barton smiled reassuringly, "Hasn't anyone told you how far we can coast with our motors shut off? There is very little danger, Timmy, because we can contact ships by radio during the entire trip. In case of emergency, we would order a ship to stand by while we landed on the lee side."

"But supposing we should run out of gas?"

"That would be practically impossible. We carry enough fuel to fly us five thousand miles. The distance to Hawaii is less than half that. Even if our radio were to fail us, we could still find our way. Every one of our officers is a skilled navigator as well as aviator. We would determine our position by the sun or stars, just as sailors do. These Clipper ships, Timmy, in reality are flying boats."

Mr. Barton walked over to the galley window and looked out. Now the sun had dropped below the rim of the ocean and all that remained was a thin margin of gold. Suddenly he called to Timmy. "Speaking of boats," he said, "we will pass one on our port side very soon."

Timmy raced back to the lounge to announce the news to some of the other passengers. As the word spread quickly through the plane, the passengers gathered at the windows to view the

approaching ship. Timmy raised the Venetian blinds so that everyone could see out. Gracefully then the Clipper Ship swooped low to salute the vessel. By now, long searchlights from the vessel's deck swept the skies in blazing streaks.

"Watch closely, Timmy," said Mr. Barton.

Obeying, Timmy saw the lights of the Clipper Ship flash off and on to signal the liner below. The lights of the vessel flashed quickly in return, and its searchlights played brilliantly across the wings of the clipper ship.

Timmy pressed his face against the window and stared into the darkening night until the lights were no longer visible.

Presently dinner was served, and he ate his savory meal with a keen appetite. When he had finished, he took a seat by the window and watched a pale winter moon creep slowly into the eastern sky. A few straggling wisps of cloud glowed in the faint light like puffs of cotton. Closing his eyes to listen to the soft hum of the motors outside, he soon dozed off to sleep.

A few minutes later, Mr. Barton roused him and led him to his made-up berth. Timmy crept in wearily and began to undress behind the dark blue curtains, taking care to hang his clothes on the convenient clothes rack. Snugly tucked under the fluffy blue blankets, he took a small black book from his bag and began to write the log of his first day of travel. Finished, he lay back upon his pillow and soon fell fast asleep.

LOGBOOK

SHIP: China Clipper, bound for China.

POSITION: Mid-Pacific Ocean, 8,000 feet high.

TIME: 9:45 P. M.

WITNESS: Timmy Blake, San Francisco, California

COMMENTS:

Weather is clear and moonlight. I think this Clipper Ship is the most wonderful plane I have ever seen. I want to be a Pilot some day. It takes about six years to be a good Pilot.

I wonder what Mother and Dad are thinking tonight? If they could only see me now! There are lots of nice people on board. That tall man with the beard looks like an explorer. Another man with a pretty wife told me he had flown to China three times already. He said I will like Midway and Wake Islands. I can spear fish under water and everything out there.

I'm too tired to write any more. Ahoy for Honolulu in the morning.

T. Blake

Adapted from *Timmy Rides the China Clipper*

Three Boys on the Subway

By Arna Bontemps

SLUMBER, his big brother, Rags, and his little brother, Willie, were visiting their uncle in Harlem. Soon after their arrival their uncle gave them each a nickel, but there were so many wonderful things to do and see in New York that the boys had a hard time deciding how to spend the money. Then came an afternoon on which the boys had nothing to do. For a while they flipped their nickels, but finally Slumber thought of something that had been in his mind since the first day they reached New York.

"What's that down-under-the-ground car what they talk about so much?" he asked suddenly.

"The subway," Rags said. "That's the name they call it."

"How much do you reckon it costs to take a ride on it?"

Rag's eyes brightened, and he wondered why none of them had thought of that question before.

"Dog my cats," he said, all excited. "You have thought up something grand, Slumber."

"What are you talking about, big shorty?" Slumber said.

"I'm talking about you and me and Willie taking a long ride on that subway train. It just costs a nickel to go there and come back."

"To go where?" Slumber asked, his face so long and sad it almost made his brothers laugh.

"To go where the subway takes you," Rags told him.

But that explanation was just too much for little Willie.

"Well, where does the subway *take* you?" he demanded.

Rags thought for a moment, then he shook his head and shrugged his shoulders.

"I don't know where the subway takes you, and I'm not bothered," he said. "I reckon it takes you anywhere you want to go, but just so long as it brings you back where you came from, I don't care where it goes. Come on with me, you all. A subway ride is just the ticket for us."

THREE BOYS ON THE SUBWAY

Slumber and Willie did not answer, but their prompt response to Rags's suggestion was evidence enough of their agreement and pleasure. Rags took Willie's hand and commenced walking so fast the little fellow almost had to run to keep up. Slumber followed a few steps behind, his hands deep in his pockets. Slumber was thinking hard as he shuffled along behind his brothers. He was trying to imagine how a down-under-the-ground car looked and how it would feel to ride on one. Slumber concluded that the subway train was one of those things you simply had to see.

They had walked three or four blocks when Rags and Willie paused at the top of the steps that led down to the underground tracks.

"Got your nickels ready?" Rags asked, looking first at Slumber, then at Willie.

"Here's mine," Willie said, taking his from his pocket.

"I got mine," Slumber whispered.

They went down the steps slowly. All the boys were puzzled by the strange layout of things in the subway station, so they took their time and noticed what other people did.

Slumber discovered that the small booth with the man sitting at the window was the place where the people got their money changed. The folks entering the trains had to pass through one of the gates in front of the booth. These would allow only one person to enter at a time and would swing open only after the person had dropped a nickel in the slot.

"Um-hunh," Slumber said aloud. "I got that old gate down pat. You put your nickel in that there place yonder. Then you push that turn-around thing that looks like a wagon wheel with four spokes in it. When the wheel spins around, in you go. I believe I can work it slick as a whistle."

"Well, you go first then," Rags said. "It isn't good to be so smart, you know."

"I'm not being smart," Slumber said, dropping his coin in the proper place. "I just got this old subway business down pat. Now, look at me. See there, I'm in. Now you come in."

Sure enough, Slumber was in. The thing that looked like a wagon wheel with four spokes made a big noise and turned just far enough to let Slumber through. Then it would not move until another coin was dropped into the slot.

"That was pretty slick how you went through there," Rags admitted. "Now watch me. Here I come."

Rags got through safely, but Slumber could see that the older boy's heart was in his mouth as he dropped the nickel in the slot. Perhaps, Slumber thought, Rags was wondering for just a moment whether or not the wheel would turn after it had his nickel safely in its box. But a moment later he saw a smile running across his brother's face. The wheel was turning.

Willie had watched it all carefully. Now it was his turn. Willie dropped his coin in the slot as his brothers had done. And when he came through the gate he was smiling.

A train of ten cars came roaring through the dark tunnel under the ground, its two small lights shining like eyes. It stopped at the platform where the boys stood. All the doors opened at once, and Slumber and Rags and Willie entered the one nearest them. Inside the car they found seats and sat trembling as it began to pull away.

Gradually the moving train gathered speed. Soon it was going almost as fast as lightning; and as it sped down there under the ground in its tunnel, the car was filled with a roaring noise. Slumber noticed that Rags was saying something, his mouth was moving, but the train made so much noise, Slumber couldn't hear a word he said.

The train came to other underground stations and at each stop people got on and off. All seemed to know where they were going. Some read newspapers as they rode. Somehow the subway seemed just like an ordinary everyday thing to them. But Slumber was so happy and excited he soon forgot about all the people who didn't know a good ride when they took one.

"Whee!" he cried, as the subway roared around a long sloping curve, reaching a terrific speed.

"I helped you to say whee!" Willie squealed.

"Turn on the speed, Mr. Subway Man," Rags shouted. "I like nothing but fast trains."

Slumber stood up and tried walking in the moving car. It was hard to keep your feet at first, but it was fun. He motioned to Rags and Willie and they followed him through the car. They walked through car after car till they reached the open door at the very front of the train. There the wind was strong, but the boys enjoyed it because they could look ahead into the dark tunnel through which the tracks ran.

After a while the train came up out of the tunnel and ran on an elevated track above the streets.

"Well, now isn't this something," Slumber said. "This old train has come up out of the ground—just when I was commencing to like it down there, too."

"Couldn't we get off and go back?" Willie asked.

"I reckon we are going to have to get off and go back sometime soon. You can't keep going this way all the time."

"You are talking sense, big shorty," Slumber said. "Let's get off next time the train stops and go back again!"

At the next station the boys got off and went to the entrance gate.

"Now how are we going to get over on the other side and catch one of them trains going back?" Rags said.

"Just go out this way," Slumber said, pushing the gate open and going through. "Then we can go downstairs and come up on that side over yonder."

Rags looked at Slumber and groaned.

"Look what you have done. You do not have the sense you were born with. Look where you are. Just look at yourself."

Slumber couldn't see anything wrong with himself.

"I thought you wanted to go back the way we came," he said.

"You crazy possum-head boy you," Rags shouted. "Don't you see you are outside and you can't come back in without another nickel. Now how are you going to get home?"

"Oh," Slumber said. "Oh . . ."

Tears were already in Willie's eyes.

"Are we going to leave Slumber here?" he asked Rags.

"I don't know what we are going to do."

But there was no need to moan now. The boys had traveled enough to know that you didn't get anywhere by standing still. You didn't go places by quarreling and grumbling.

"I've got to get home, some kind of way," Slumber said.

"And I expect we'd best come the same way," Rags said.

He and Willie pushed through the gates—they turned very easily when you were coming out—and followed the sad Slumber down the steps to the ground.

"I don't know where I'm at, and I don't know which way is home," Slumber murmured. "But if ever I get back to Harlem, I'll know more about traveling on that old subway train next time. That's a tricky old something-or-another-way they got them subway gates fixed up. You are just as apt to get yourself locked out as you are to get locked in."

They were walking down a paved highway, Slumber playing a tune on his harmonica, when a taxicab stopped at the curb and honked at them.

"Say, aren't you all Harlem boys?" the driver called.

"Yes, suh," Slumber called back. "We sure are Harlem boys and we are aiming to get back home the best way we can."

"Come on hop in then," the driver said. "I'm a Harlem taxi driver. I just happened to drive somebody way out this way, and I'd just as soon carry you three back with me as not."

"Much obliged," the boys said, getting into the cab. "We are sure proud to get a ride home."

"You say you're Harlem boys?"

"Well, suh," Slumber said, trying to explain a little better, "I was just beginning to think we were Harlem boys, but after what happened to us this afternoon, I kind of think we are still Alabama boys."

The cab driver laughed as they told him how Slumber had

got off the subway and left the gate before noticing that it was not possible to come back in without another coin. He agreed with them that they were not really Harlem boys. But he thought that did not matter, because they all seemed to be very good-humored and amusing Alabama boys.

Night came while they were on the way home. All the street lights were on when the cab stopped in front of their home.

Uncle Jasper Tappin was smoking a pipe in the basement entrance when he saw the cab door open and the boys get out. For a moment he thought he must have been dreaming.

The boys were giggling proudly as they met him. But Uncle Jasper Tappin could not imagine what had happened or how they could arrange to come home in such fine style.

"Dog my cats," he said, shaking his old head. "You three are the beatingest set of boys that ever I *did* see."

Adapted from *The Sad-Faced Boy*

Uncle Harry and the Aunts

By Caroline D. Emerson

UNCLE HARRY and the aunts were coming for Christmas! Everybody in the Marshall family was busy getting ready. Mother was stuffing the turkey. Nan was polishing the extra teaspoons. Jimmie was taking out the ashes from the fireplace and bringing up more wood. A trail of ashes across the floor was all he had to show so far.

Jimmie stopped to tell Nan how to polish the spoons.

"No, Nan is getting on nicely," said mother, as she urged Jimmie away from the pantry and toward the cellar door.

Nan was perched on a high stool. She was growing tall. She had been six on her last birthday and she had started school in September. Her seventh birthday was soon to come. Her dark hair hung in two braids on either side of her face and her brown eyes were open just as wide as ever.

Jimmie looked much the same as he had looked for some time. His eyes were blue and his hair sandy yellow. His nose was covered with freckles. No one ever would have supposed that Nan and Jimmie were brother and sister.

When the spoons were finished, Nan and Jimmie cracked the nuts. While they worked they whispered together in excitement. There was a surprise in store for Uncle Harry and the aunts. The workmen had been at the Marshall house again. Father had had another big improvement put in. They were the first people in all the town to have it. And that night, that very night, "IT" was to be turned on!

"Any one want to drive to the station with me to meet the people?" called father.

There was a scurry for coats and mufflers and overshoes. Nan knew just where her things were, but Jimmie emptied the closet hunting for his. While mother picked up stray overshoes and shut the closet door after Jimmie, Nan and Jimmie raced out the front door. By the mounting block stood a sleigh with two bay horses waiting impatiently in front of it. Mr. Marshall took the reins from the driver and climbed in. Nan and Jimmie bundled in beside him and father tucked the buffalo robe about them. It was a crisp cold day and the sun was nearly ready to set.

The bells of the sleigh began to tinkle. Off the sleigh dashed toward the town. There were many sleighs hitched in front of the stores, for people were out doing last-minute Christmas shopping. Everyone seemed happy and gay. Nan wanted to sing for joy. Her shopping was done. She had a present for father and mother and one for Jimmie hidden safely at home.

Down at the station there were a few people waiting, and the village hack was drawn up by the steps.

"Train is twenty minutes late," said the stationmaster.

"Trains on this line are always twenty minutes late," laughed father.

"If they aren't still later," grumbled the hackman, who had to meet all the trains.

"We'll go for a longer drive," said father.

Along the snowy road the horses trotted. The bells jingled and the sleigh slid so smoothly that it seemed to Nan as if they were flying. Down a steep hill they went. There were boys sliding who had to stand to one side in the deep snow to let the sleigh pass. Jimmie waved to his friends. On the trip back Mr. Marshall gave them a ride up the hill.

"Merry Christmas!" shouted Nan to them as they untied their sleds at the top of the hill.

"Merry Christmas!" they all shouted. Then off went the sleigh with snow flying from the horses' heels. Back at the station there was still no train. Nan went into the stuffy waiting room to warm herself by the stove. A dim lamp hung from the ceiling. Nan looked at it in amusement.

"Do you suppose 'IT' will be turned on when we get home?" she asked Jimmie. "It's getting dark."

Just then came the distant whistle of the train far down the track. Nan and Jimmie ran out onto the platform. Father had to stay with the horses. The train grew larger and noisier. Then in it came with a rush and a roar that made Nan press back against the wall of the station. The steaming monster came to a halt. Off jumped Mr. Robinson, who had been conductor on that train since before Nan was born. Soon Uncle Harry stepped out on the platform. His white mustache stuck out above the corners of his fur collar and made him look like a friendly walrus. Nan waved to him and shouted.

Soon the aunts appeared behind. Mr. Robinson helped them down the steps. The aunts kissed Nan and cooed over her and said what a big girl she was getting to be. Jimmie helped Uncle Harry carry the bags around to the sleigh.

The sleigh was filled to overflowing, but at last everyone was tucked in with all the bags and the baggage. Mr. Marshall clucked to the horses and off they dashed toward home.

Nan kept looking ahead with impatience. At last they turned the corner by the Marshall house.

"Now watch out!" cried Nan to the aunts.

"Look out for what, Nan?" asked one of the aunts mildly.

"Oh, oh!" cried Nan, for just at that minute the surprise happened.

The other houses along the street were lighted here and there by lamps that sent a soft light through the windows. But suddenly as they watched, the Marshall house leaped into a blaze of lights, so that the other houses seemed like pale, distant stars beside it. The parlor windows gleamed brilliantly. The dining-room windows were quite as bright. The upstairs hall window shone and all the four windows in each of the bedrooms were aglow.

"Is the house on fire?" cried the littlest

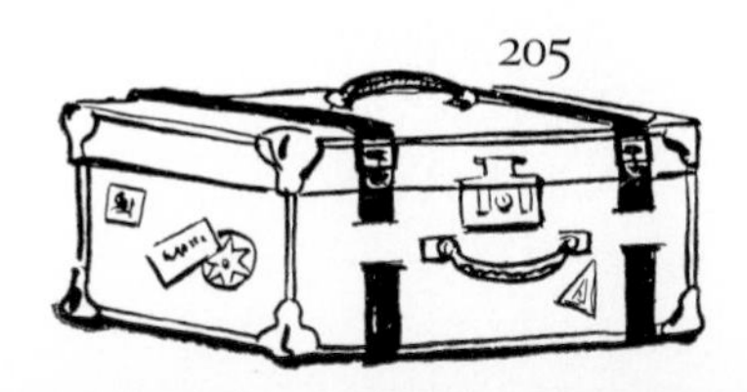

aunt in dismay. "James, James, what has happened?"

They expected to see father leap from the sleigh and rush down the street, shouting "FIRE" at the top of his lungs. But he did nothing of the sort. He pulled the horses to a stop and sat looking.

"That's what electricity can do," he said. "That is what one would call a real improvement!"

Jimmie could hardly wait to jump out and run into the house, but the excitement of the moment kept him still. Nan took long breaths of the cold air and her eyes shone as though they too had little electric lights in them. Then the front door opened in a flood of light and mother's voice came across the snow.

"Aren't you people ever coming in?" she called gaily.

Father drove the team in at the gate and they all clambered out with much laughing and calling of merry Christmases.

Inside Jimmie and Nan rushed, and began turning on and off the lights. It was like magic. One second the room was as dark as a pocket. The next second you could see to pick up a pin in any corner. Nan looked at the little wires that ran across the ceiling and carried this new electricity.

"I thought they'd swell up when the electricity came into them," said Nan. "But they are just as little as ever."

"Oh, no," said Jimmie scornfully, "wires don't swell up."

He knew as little about it as Nan, but he didn't like to admit it. But one thing Jimmie had found out. He pointed at the delicate glass bulb that hung at the end of the cord.

"If you drop one of those, or break it in any way, it goes off like Fourth of July," announced Jimmie.

Nan stroked the glass softly. It looked to her like a frozen soap bubble with fairy wires within, but Nan always had strange fancies about things. "Nan's nonsense," Jimmie called it. He wanted to know how things worked.

From *Father's Big Improvements*

Joyce Ballantyne

Steam Comes Upriver

By Josephine E. Phillips

JONATHAN rubbed his eyes awake and peered out through a chink in the thick log wall. Then he rolled off his bunk and began scrambling into his clothes.

"Sally!" he called to his sister, asleep in the cabin loft above. "Sally! The river's bank-full! Today the great boat may come upstream! Hurry! After the chores we'll watch for it."

"Will it really come today?" she squealed.

Jonathan nodded, gulping. "All that's kept it back was the water not being up. Now this freshet has come. Just think! A steamboat on our own Muskingum! Hooray!"

"But the current may be too strong," their mother warned. "The boat may fail—"

"It can't fail! It mustn't!" Jonathan told her. He donned heavy jacket and coonskin cap, and picked up the milk pail. "I just wish I could boost it along, though."

"You'd better be thinking about boosting some breakfast for old Dan, and about milking the cow," Mother laughed.

Jonathan ran first to the riverbank and stood there daydreaming for a while. How wonderful it would be to see the fine, broad-decked *Rufus Putnam,* with its little swivel cannon and its tall chimney stack, come steaming around the bend!

Already there were boats with engines that chewed wood and puffed smoke and turned paddlewheels along the broad Ohio. But a swift-running river like the Muskingum, some said, would never let itself be conquered by an engine. Others, though, shook their heads wisely. Hadn't steamboats sailed on the Hudson for fifteen years now? And hadn't the steamer, *The Savannah,* been built to journey over the wide Atlantic?

His thoughts were rudely interrupted by the sound of galloping hoofs.

"The *Rufus Putnam* is on her way!" the rider shouted. "She left Marietta yesterday. Tied up for the night at Luke's Chute—is on her way again now—hopes to make Zanesville before dark."

"B-but d-didn't she r-run aground or anything?" Jonathan stammered in his excitement.

"Not a thing! Her only trouble is in getting enough firewood. Yesterday they stopped a dozen times and sent men ashore to cut trees. That's why I'm riding ahead now, to ask farmers along the river to have fuel ready. Captain Greene will pay them well." The man wheeled and cantered away.

Jonathan almost stumbled into his milk pail. He stopped at the cabin long enough to tell Mother and Sally about the messenger, then ran to the stable. At sight of old Dan, whinnying greeting, Jonathan had a sudden idea.

He would let Captain Greene have the firewood piled by their cabin door, just as Father would do, if he were home. But he would do more. All autumn he had worked during his spare time in Widow Amos' timber lot. There were several sled loads now, of the small maple and beech growth he had felled. That was what he and old Dan could do to help the steamboat. It would help Widow Amos, too, for ready money was scarce, and whatever Captain Greene might offer would be very welcome.

He finished the milking quickly and harnessed Dan. At the cabin door Sally met him, clad in warm deerskin coat and leggings, and a cap that matched his own.

"Good!" she cried, hurrying to seat herself on the huge wood

sled. "You thought of Widow Amos' timber too! And Mother says I may help you load. I'm not big, like Cyrus Maxon, but I'm willing-er. And I don't have a lame shoulder the way he usually does, if there's work to be done."

They set off eagerly. The lumber road was barely more than a rough trail, but the snow covered the worst bumps, and Dan, a frontier horse, was used to such traveling. They reached the woodpiles and commenced loading.

Sally tugged and lifted with him, but she had not a man's strength and the task took longer than expected. When they had put on as much as Dan could haul, they turned homeward.

They found Cyrus Maxon sitting on their doorstep, and his horse, Jericho, tied to their hitching post.

"Hear about the steamboat?" Jonathan called.

Cyrus nodded, grinning. "That's why I'm here. Pap and I haven't much wood. Thought I'd like to watch her load yours on."

"That's fine. Come and help us drop these over by the sycamore. It'll be the handiest place for her to pull up to. And maybe we can haul another load, before she comes."

Cyrus shook his head. "Don't count much on me, loading or unloading. My shoulder's lame. There's no rush about the firewood, anyhow, I figure. What they don't pick up here they can get farther along." He strolled after the sled. Occasionally he helped unload a stick. Mostly he just stood.

They left him just standing when they started back.

"Better wait," he warned. "Seems as if I heard her coming. Better stay here."

But Jonathan and Sally heard nothing. They stopped old Dan to listen, but there was only the silence of the winter forest.

They reached the heaps of wood and set to work once more.

"I guess somebody's shoulders will be lame tomorrow," Jonathan told his puffing, red-faced sister.

"I shan't care—tomorrow," she replied with a laugh.

They surveyed their second load proudly. A pretty purseful it would mean to Widow Amos.

"And real help to the *Rufus Putnam,*" Sally reminded him.

"Giddap!" they clucked.

Dan started.

"Whoa!" Jonathan suddenly halted him.

There was, indeed, something in the air now—a heavy, throbbing sound they had never heard. The engine! The steamboat must be nearing the bend!

"Giddap!" Jonathan shouted excitedly.

At the same moment the roar of a small cannon burst on their ears. Such a thunder had not rung through the forest since the days of the old fort. Dan reared at the unfamiliar sound. He started to run. The loaded sled dragged on him. He swerved, grazing a stump, then stumbled. His left hind foot caught in a heap of loose stones and he came to a quivering standstill.

"There!" Sally stood at his head and spoke reassuringly, while Jonathan tried to free him. In a moment they discovered that Dan had not only scuffed a good bit of hide from his leg, but that a sharp stone had lodged so firmly in his hoof that no amount of ordinary prying would loosen it.

The sound of the steam engine pounded in their ears. Should they leave old Dan there while they themselves ran to view the boat? Then how would they get the fuel to the riverbank?

"Run, Sally, and ask Cyrus to bring Jericho, to hitch on in place of Dan. We'll hobble along and meet him."

Sally ran. She had never run faster. Queerly, though, the steam engine thud pounded less and less loudly. When she reached the clearing there was only a plume of pale black smoke drifting over the river. The woodpile by their cabin door had vanished. There was no Cyrus, no Jericho, in sight.

"Mother! Mother!" she burst into the cabin. "Has the steamboat come and gone already?"

Mother nodded. "But Cyrus is following it along the river on horseback. I thought you and Jonathan could jump on Dan and do the same, so as not to miss seeing—"

"But we have missed it! We've missed it entirely!" wailed Sally. "Dan has picked up a stone, so he's lame. We couldn't hurry. He took fright at the cannon."

"Dan got coltish and tried to run away? Dear! Dear!" Mother had to laugh, and so did Sally when she thought about it, their aged Dan trying to act frightened. "I guess nothing short of a cannon could do that! But you and Jonathan won't feel so badly when you know Captain Greene is to stop on his way back from Zanesville, on Tuesday if all goes well. You can see the boat then, and he will pay for the wood."

With that promise and, later in the afternoon, Cyrus' glowing

description of the *Rufus Putnam,* the two had to be satisfied. Sally thought Tuesday would never come.

Jonathan was so worried about Dan that he hardly had time to think. His best efforts at getting out the stone did not succeed. The injury was deep, so that soon the horse's leg was swollen almost to the hock. The boy used all the good healing herbs and poultices, but in vain. There was no horse doctor, and even the blacksmith was off down river with a load.

What would Father say, when he returned? There was no money for replacing old Dan—and no horse anywhere that they could love as much.

Early Tuesday afternoon Jonathan was working over his patient when Sally called, "Something's coming! There's smoke beyond the treetops!"

Soon they heard the rumble of engine and paddlewheel, and the big boat drew into sight, splashing and chugging. Jonathan could not take his eyes from it. He forgot old Dan, forgot Sally, forgot everything. This was so different from what he had thought. Citizens of Marietta, which was almost forty miles away, crowded the deck. The boy was almost as thrilled to see them as to watch the steamer itself as it nosed clumsily up, alongside the sycamore. Marietta must be a very grand place. He had been taken there on a visit once, when he was too tiny to remember.

"Well, young fellow!" Captain Greene hailed him. "Got some more wood for us?"

"Some," Jonathan nodded, pointing.

The Captain came ashore, looked the fuel over, and counted out the cash to pay for it and what he had taken before.

"You didn't get around in time to see us the other day, did

you? Want to come aboard, both of you?" He waved Jonathan and Sally toward the plank that led to the deck.

Gingerly, but full of excitement and curiosity, the two mounted and were shown about. They saw the cabin and the freight hold; the hot, stuffy, wood-smoke-smudged engine room, and the shelves that answered as beds. They saw the cannon and heard how it had been fired so many times in Zanesville that hardly a whole pane of glass was left along the river front! The passengers were delighted to explain everything and they finished by saying, "No matter how grand it looks, it's nothing compared to how you feel, to go swooping along the water in it."

Captain Greene had taken a liking to Jonathan and his sister, and asked, "How about making the run to Marietta with us?"

Jonathan's eyes got very big, and Sally's mouth went into a big round *O*. Then Jonathan swallowed and shook his head.

"Don't you want to? Afraid?"

"Oh, yes, sir. That is, no, sir. That is—I can't very well—go. I can't leave old Dan. You see—" With Sally's help, Jonathan explained about drawing the firewood for Widow Amos and for the steamer, about the stone and the swollen hind leg, and the blacksmith being away. "Sally can go with you, if Mother is willing, but I must stay and take care of Dan."

"Hm!" declared Captain Greene. "We have a good horse doctor right in Marietta. And I'm really responsible for Dan's going lame. Why don't you pile him aboard and we'll take him

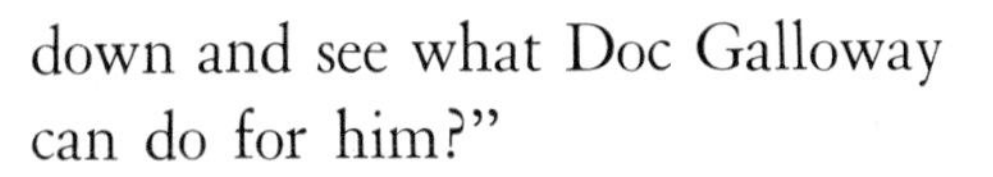

down and see what Doc Galloway can do for him?"

"Oh, oh, thank you!" The generosity of this offer almost took Jonathan's breath away. He forgot that with Father away he could not well leave the cabin and its hard chores to Mother. When he remembered, he explained, "B——but, sir. I——I guess I'll have to stay here. Perhaps Sally can see about Dan—"

"Not alone, she couldn't." A familiar voice interrupted him. He turned and saw Cyrus Maxon. Cyrus must have just come aboard in time to hear Captain Greene's offer. "I'm really responsible about Dan. I ought to have helped you load the other day. If you'll take him down to Marietta to get his leg fixed, I'll see that your mother's chores are done. My shoulder isn't lame today. I don't think it's going to bother any more ever. I want to be a steamboat engineer like Si Dow. He says it's hard work and a fellow wants to start getting up steam for it before he gets any older than I. You and Sally and Dan go along in the *Rufus Putnam*. I'll see to things here."

And suddenly Sally and Jonathan saw that steam had come upriver in more ways than one!

Six Days on an Ocean Liner

By Henry B. Lent

NOW, at last, the sailing day has come! How excited the passengers are as they walk down the pier toward the gangplanks of the big ocean liner.

Let us go up. Wait a minute! First show your passport and ticket to the officer here in the booth on the pier. Every passenger must do this before starting up the gangplank. The officer inspects each passport and each ticket. Then he tears off part of the ticket. Now we may go up. People who are going aboard only to say good-by to their friends do not have to show a passport or ticket.

From the end of the gangplank we step onto the main deck of the liner. It is getting close to sailingtime, but first of all we shall find our cabin and make sure that everything is all right. A steward meets us. He looks at our tickets.

"Cabin Twenty-five A," he says. "This way, please."

We follow him through a doorway from the main promenade deck into the main hall, or foyer, of the liner. All around us people are saying good-by to their friends. Everyone seems eager for the sailing. The ship's orchestra is playing. Porters and stewards rush to and fro with bags and packages.

Our steward takes us down a wide, curved stairway onto

deck A. We walk down a long corridor past many cabin doors. Each door has a number on it. Here is cabin Twenty-five. The steward opens the door for us. This is the room in which we shall live during our three-thousand-mile voyage across the ocean.

What a surprise! It looks just as comfortable as the rooms at home! There are two real beds, and look over there on that dressing table. There are packages, letters, and telegrams. They all have your name on them. Even though your friends could not come to New York to see you sail, they have not forgotten you. These are "bon-voyage" presents which they have sent, wishing you a pleasant voyage. Here is a big basket of fruit, all wrapped in cellophane. Beside it are three books to read. Someone has even sent you a box of paints.

Let us look about the cabin a bit before we go on deck. There are comfortable chairs to sit in, and wardrobes in which to hang our clothes. A large mirror is over each dressing table.

The door at the farther end of the cabin opens into a small private bathroom. In it is a spotless white bathtub with a shower over it. Everything, in fact, is just as you would wish it.

The walls of the cabin are made of beautiful polished woods of different colors. The ceiling, too, is inlaid with wood in the form of a design.

Over each bed are two buttons. One is marked "Stewardess." The stewardess is the maid who will take care of our cabin, make our beds, and bring us things we may need. If mother and sister were here, the stewardess would take care of all their needs. The other button is marked "Steward." The steward is the man who will shine our shoes, care for our clothes, and see that we are always comfortable. Whenever we want anything, all we have to do is ring one of these electric buzzers.

Instead of portholes, our cabin has square windows. *Portholes,* used on most of the lower decks, are round with thick glass. They can be closed tightly in rough weather. If they are even slightly opened, waves may wash against them and water may come into the cabin. We are so high up that we shall doubtless keep our windows open. At sea we shall be able to look through them far out over the ocean.

When we go up on the main deck again, there is even more bustle than before. One of the ship's officers walks along the deck, calling as he goes, "All ashore that are going ashore! All ashore that are going ashore!"

Let us go over to the deck railing with the other passengers who are waving to friends on the pier. Two minutes left! The men on the pier are beginning to unfasten the heavy ropes that hold the gangplanks. Everything must be ready, for an ocean liner leaves right on the dot, just as a train does.

Twelve o'clock. The deep rumble of the liner's whistle drowns out all other noises. Hum-m-m-m! This is to let everybody know that the liner is starting, and to warn all the small river boats to keep out of the way.

The men on the pier pull back the gangplanks. Other men slip off the big ropes and cables that hold the liner fast to the pier. We cannot talk now, because the roar of the liner's whistle

is making so much noise.

Handkerchiefs flutter. Hands and hats wave in the air. Good-by! Good-by! The liner is moving, stern first, out into the Hudson River.

Deep down in the engine rooms of the ocean liner the engines start throbbing. For six whole days and nights they must work without resting, turning the huge propellers that drive the liner through the water. For the first few hours the engines will run only at half speed, for there is danger of bumping into one of the many river boats that cross our path.

Here we go, on our way down the river toward the outer harbor and the broad Atlantic Ocean. More than three thousand miles of water. Think of it! We shall not see any land for five days—almost a week. And then we shall be off the coast of England, on our way to France.

Some of the passengers, as soon as they had come aboard the liner and found their own cabins, went to the dining room to select the table they liked best. The table they choose for the first meal is the one they will sit at during every meal for the rest of the voyage. As we walk down the beautiful curved stairway into the dining room, the head waiter meets us.

"There is a lovely table over there, right by a porthole," he tells us.

Yes, we shall take that one, for then we can look out over the water as we dine. There is a card on the white tablecloth which says "Table No. 67." This will be our table during the rest of the voyage.

Just for fun, let your hand wander under the tablecloth. Feel along the under edge of the table and you will notice something interesting. On each side of every table is a narrow rack, or frame, that rises when you push it up. Do you know why? In rough weather, the waiter raises these racks to prevent the dishes from sliding off onto the floor.

A liner as large as ours is so steady that this is seldom necessary. Passengers on smaller ships, however, often have to raise this useful little "fence" around the plates and dishes. And, in winter, when the ocean is rough and stormy, even people on large liners must use these racks.

There are several hundred passengers at dinner. If it were not for the round portholes, we might think we were in the dining room of a big hotel. There is soft carpet on the floor. At one end of the dining room are many palms and even growing vines. On each table is a vase of flowers.

And such food to select for dinner! A king and queen might well be pleased to choose the dishes for their dinner from the delicious foods that are listed on the gaily decorated menu! There is everything you could possibly wish for, and many other things you have never even thought of wishing for.

Having breakfast, lunch, and dinner every day on an ocean liner is lots of fun.

It also is fun wandering about the liner, watching the men at their work. During our days on shipboard we visit the boiler rooms and engine rooms and other parts. We talk with mem-

bers of the crew and with some of the ship's officers. The captain, of course, is in charge. He is the most important man on an ocean liner. He is in full command of the ship and of all the people on her, even the passengers. All the ship's officers, and the men in her crew, must do exactly as he says.

No matter what happens, it is his job to see that the ocean liner sails safely across the Atlantic. If she should have an accident, and sink, he would be the last man to leave her.

But perhaps we have been missing some fun on deck. Let us spend some time seeing what the other passengers are doing.

There are many beautiful social rooms and halls on our liner, all for the special use of the passengers.

The library, for instance, is a very pleasant place to spend an hour or two. Rows of books line the walls, books for boys and girls as well as for grownups. There is a librarian in charge of this room.

The grand salon is one of the largest and most beautiful rooms on the ship. With its thick soft carpet, and its beautiful drapes and furniture, it is almost like the lobby of a magnificent hotel. This is where the ship's concerts are given. On Sunday this room becomes a chapel. The passengers gather here for the regular

Sunday-morning church service.

Near by is the lounge. This, too, is a beautiful room. In the center is a glass dance floor, where people dance in the afternoon and evening. Right now the ship's orchestra is playing a lively tune from one of Broadway's newest shows. Several couples are on the floor, dancing. Others sit at tables, having their afternoon tea, talking and laughing. It is just like a party, isn't it?

Many of the passengers are sitting in their deck chairs out on the promenade deck. Some have rugs wrapped about them and are fast asleep. Others are reading or talking to their neighbors. It is interesting to watch the people who walk by, round and round the deck, chatting as they go. Everyone seems quite gay.

It is all very well for some people to think that it is most fun just to sit in their deck chairs, resting. As for us, we must find something more exciting to do.

How about a horseback ride? Did you know that there was a horse on board? He is an electric horse. Here he is in the gymnasium, over in the corner. Climb into the saddle. Hold on tightly. Now turn this switch. There he goes, rocking back and forth. How do you like that? It is good exercise.

The ship's gymnasium is really a wonderful exercise room.

SIX DAYS ON AN OCEAN LINER

There are dumbbells, weight-lifting machines, boxing gloves, punching bags, and even rowing machines. Up on the sun deck some of the passengers have started a game of shuffleboard. They push the round wooden disks, trying to make them go into one of the squares which have been painted on the deck. One of them scoots across the deck and stops in the square marked 10.

"That's ten points for me!" shouts one of the players. The next one slides right into the 100 square. That was lucky!

In the children's playroom there is a Punch and Judy show. Many grownups are watching, too. Have you ever seen a Punch and Judy show? It is a lot of fun to see the little puppets go through their antics.

Two stewards really run the show. They both crawl into the booth out of sight and make the puppets seem very much alive. Bang! The funny little policeman with the long red nose hits Punch over the head with his club. Bang! Bang! Bang! Everyone laughs at the amusing pranks of Punch and the other actors in the show.

There is always something for the passengers to do to amuse themselves on a ship at sea. Tonight there will be a concert by the ship's orchestra. Then comes a ping-pong match to see who is the champion player on board the ship. *Ping-pong* is like tennis, played on a large table marked out in courts.

Now that we are way out at sea, how would you like to send a message back home to Billy? To do that we must go to the wireless office on deck *B*. We shall send a radiogram.

The clerk gives us pencil and paper. Put down Billy's full name and his address. Then write what you want to say to him. That's fine. Now the radio operator will send your message out over the liner's radio, or wireless, through the air. The radio man in New York will receive the message. Bill will have it in an hour or two.

It is wonderful to think that an ocean liner so far out at sea can send messages back to New York, or ahead to Europe, in a few hours' time. The messages travel through a thousand miles or more of space. We can also "talk" by means of these wireless messages to other ships at sea, even though they are too far away to be seen.

More wonderful still—on some ocean liners it is possible for a passenger to step into a special telephone booth and talk to a friend anywhere in the whole world over this telephone. The words he says are carried through the air over the ocean by radio, and then sent over regular land telephone wires to his friend's telephone in Chicago, San Francisco, or wherever it may be.

And now, after nearly a week at sea, our voyage is coming to an end. We are within sight of the coast of France. The town nestling at the foot of the hill is Havre. The early morning sunlight glistens on the windows of the little white houses. A winding road leads back up over the steep hill.

We must go inside now, for just a few minutes. All the passengers are going into the main hall of the liner for passport inspection. One by one we file past a table where two men are sitting. These men inspect each passport. They tell us that our passports are all right. They give us a *landing card.* No one may leave the ship without this landing card.

Finally both bow and stern of the liner are tied snug and fast alongside the pier. Now the gangplanks have been made fast. Hang on tightly to your landing card, for you must hand it to the officer at the end of the gangplank. Here we go, down the gangplank onto the pier.

Although we have many wonderful new sights to look forward to, where we are going, we feel a little sad to be leaving our ocean liner. For almost a week we have had such fun living in this marvelous "floating city."

Now she stands, tied fast to the pier. We know that already everyone is busy on board, getting her ready for her next voyage back across the Atlantic. Day after tomorrow, the band will play again, the passengers will come aboard, the captain will take his position on the bridge, the officers and crew will work and keep watch, and the great liner will head back across the ocean toward New York.

As we look back for a final glimpse, tiny wisps of smoke curl upward from her three funnels.

Adapted from *Full Steam Ahead*

All Aboard the DeWitt Clinton

By Jeannette Covert Nolan

DEREK was in the crowd pressing through the Albany streets that hot summer morning. At the foot of the incline which led upward, he faltered—he couldn't quite remember whether he had promised Grandmother not to mount to the mysterious place at the top.

But the people at his heels kept him from turning back. With short, sturdy legs he climbed. At the crest, he saw the men, women, and children who were, like himself, to be mere observers of this modern miracle; and also those lucky few who were to have a part in it. And he saw the iron horse!

There it was, the demon machine, puffing, panting on the track: the engine, DeWitt Clinton, which today (God willing!) would haul its load over the steel rails the tremendous distance from Albany to Schenectady, and all the way back.

Grandmother had said the trip simply couldn't be made—not without catastrophe; Grandfather was as skeptical. It seemed, though, that other people had faith in the engine.

Well, Derek would watch and learn.

The DeWitt Clinton was not large, but it had enormous wheels and a smokestack rearing loftily above a central dome. An important-looking person stood on a tiny platform behind the locomotive; his job was to operate and steer the train. Behind the engineer, a small car held a pile of wood and two barrels of water draped with a leather hose; and then came three conveyances like the bodies of stagecoaches, linked to the fuel wagon and to each other by lengths of chain. Each coach would accommodate a number of occupants, with additional seats outside. Attached to the final coach was a string of flatcars, intended for freight or baggage, but set today with benches for the guests invited to take the tour.

Derek noticed all the details of the train. Strolling, he trod on the toes of someone's elegant boots and felt a firm hand grasp his shoulder.

"Hi, youngster! Do that again and you'll spoil a masterpiece!"

"Excuse me, sir." Derek glanced up apologetically.

The owner of the boots and the voice was tall, fashionably dressed, bareheaded. In the crook of his left arm, the man balanced his beaver hat. He was sketching on a paper spread over the hat crown, his eyes flicking from the paper to the coaches, the flatcars, with the regularity of a clock's pendulum. His face was weathered, but pleasant.

"What are you drawing, sir?" Derek pulled at the man's coat.

"What do you suppose?" Without interruption, the artist wielded his pencil. "You realize, perhaps, that this August ninth, 1831, is an historic occasion?"

"Because of the train?"

"Precisely. The story of the first official trip of the DeWitt Clinton will be written into the annals of our glorious America —and with it, the name of William Brown."

"Are you William Brown?"

"At your service." The man bowed. "And you?"

"Derek Dexter. I'm ten. I live in Albany with my grandparents."

"You're a passenger for Schenectady?"

"Oh, no!" Derek grinned. "I'd love to go, but I can't. But tell me, are you going, sir?"

"I wouldn't miss it for the world!" Mr. Brown thrust the paper into the pocket of his brocade waistcoat. "Yonder bench is mine. You have my permission to sit there for a moment—just for fun!"

Soon Derek was perched on the flatcar. Around him bobbed the passengers, dignified gentlemen in whiskers and plush hats, ladies in voluminous skirts with parasols and flowery bonnets. The captain of the train was busily collecting fares. He spoke to Mr. Brown, who gestured toward Derek. Then the captain clambered to a stool in the fuel wagon.

"There have been other long railroad excursions, Derek," Mr. Brown said, sauntering to the flatcar and sitting down beside the boy. "Chiefly in the South. But never one in New York state so interesting as this. I recall—"

The blast of a tin whistle drowned all conversation; sudden tension gripped travelers and spectators. Derek leaped to his feet. "I must get off, Mr. Brown!"

The whistle shrilled again; the engine wheezed and grunted and, with a terrific lurch, rolled, the wheels revolving. As the slack in the chains was taken up, the coaches rolled, too, reluctantly, one at a time, and then the flatcars.

The result was dire confusion. Coaches and cars collided and bumped; every passenger was dislodged, thrown into the lap of the person behind him. Men roared astonished protests; women gasped or shrieked in horror. The engineer tottered and clung to his throttle. The captain, clutching an iron bar, was suspended in space like a monkey on a trapeze.

But the train moved forward. It proceeded—and what could Derek, picking himself up from the tangle of people and overturned benches, do to check it?

Mr. Brown was up and gallantly assisting other people to rise and settle themselves. Derek tugged at Mr. Brown's wrist.

"I must get off! I told Grandmother—"

Before the words were fairly out of his mouth, the engine belched forth showers of sparks from the giant smokestack. The wind was carrying the sparks in a fiery deluge which dropped upon the ladies' fluffy clothing, the silky, flowing whiskers of the men. Cotton cloth flared into jets of crimson, wool smoldered. A beautiful bonnet shot into flames and was snatched from the head of its terrified wearer.

Everyone was in a panic. Derek pounded Mr. Brown's blazing shirt collar; Mr. Brown vigorously pommeled Derek.

But the train went on. The engineer resolutely sent his iron steed over the rails.

The shower of sparks did not cease, but it diminished. All the passengers had been badly singed; their garments were comical, so tattered and blackened. In spite of this, they laughed. They had expected an adventure, and they could become accustomed to the dodging necessary to prevent serious damage.

Only Derek was sober. With every minute he was farther from Albany. Grandmother would be searching for him, worried and perhaps angry. What could he do?

Mr. Brown had an idea. "Several miles from here," he said, "we'll stop to replenish the water supply. There'll be a farm near by. You can hire a horse and gallop back to Albany."

"I haven't any money, sir."

"I'll lend you the money."

Derek thanked Mr. Brown. But it was a gloomy prospect. Even with the best horse in the county, he'd be hours getting home! He peered anxiously at the ribbon of track, straining to catch a glimpse of the water tank.

Ah, there it was!

The engineer had been doubtful of his brakes; when the water tank loomed into view, he applied them. What happened then was an exact repetition of the starting order—but in reverse.

The engine balked and was banged by the fuel wagon; the coaches rocked together; the trailing flatcars crashed and jolted. The whole train shuddered convulsively and stopped.

With Mr. Brown leading, the men and boys among the passengers tumbled out and began tearing down a rail fence at the roadside. Mr. Brown said the rails must be wedged between the cars to avoid the perils of starting and stopping.

"Who'll volunteer to help me?" cried Mr. Brown.

Derek volunteered—he would have been a deserter not to! Like a little Trojan he labored, and by the time the rails were all in place the captain had tooted his whistle, and the courageous travelers were scrambling aboard again.

Easily, without jarring a bit, the train was off!

"The worst is past," Mr. Brown said consolingly to Derek. "Isn't this comfortable?"

"I ought to be at home," grumbled Derek.

"You ought," agreed the artist, smiling. "But what can't be cured must be endured. So why not be happy? I'll guarantee that fifty years from today, you'll have no regrets."

Derek considered the advice. He couldn't be *quite* happy. And yet the riding was lots of fun!

After that pause at the water tank, the DeWitt Clinton chugged triumphantly through the open fields where astonished cattle eyed it distrustfully. Frightened colts neighed, dogs barked madly, and farmers leaned on their plows to stare. At crossroads, knots of villagers cheered the train. At Schenectady, more than a thousand citizens were assembled in a welcoming committee. During the two-hour interval, there were enthusiastic speeches, waving flags, and refreshments of cooling drinks and delicious pastries.

By comparison with the outward trip, the return to Albany was uneventful. The passengers said that the railroad was proving its worth; it had come to stay, to speed the development of a growing nation. They laughed and joked and sang.

As the engine braked at the incline, Derek was silent.

"Do you want me to escort you to your grandmother, Derek?"

Mr. Brown asked. "To explain?"

"No, sir." He shook his head. "Good-by."

"Well!" said Grandmother, looking up as he stepped in the door. "So you went on a journey?" She wore her gold-rimmed spectacles and was reading the newspaper, the Albany *Argus*.

"I—I didn't mean to, ma'am. But," he said honestly, "I did enjoy it."

"Didn't mean to? Why, that wandering artist fellow paid your fare. Deacon Pierce was on the platform and overheard him talking to the train captain about you."

Derek gulped. It hadn't occurred to him! What a whimsical thing for Mr. Brown to do! But he'd only intended to be kind.

"Your grandfather is at the hotel now," Grandmother said, "to reimburse the artist. We Dexters don't accept such favors. We pay our own way. Your dinner's on the table. I saved it for you."

Derek dawdled over the milk and gingerbread. He wasn't hungry, he'd eaten heartily at Schenectady. Then Grandfather came in.

"I've been to see Brown." Grandfather sat down. He was bluff and snowy-bearded. "He says you weren't a truant, Derek. You had no suspicion of the little trick he played on you."

"No, sir. I hadn't."

"Brown says he thought it would be a treat, a fine experience for a lad of ten. And I guess he's right. A tale for you to tell your children that you rode on the first train running between the two cities of Albany and Schenectady." Grandfather stroked his beard. "You know what the artist's done?"

"What?" demanded Grandmother, seating herself beside her husband.

"He made a sketch of the DeWitt Clinton and now he's cut a silhouette of it out of black paper. It's good. Remarkable! I declare you can recognize the passengers, everyone! Brown plans to exhibit his silhouette all over New England and then present it to the Connecticut Historical Society."

"My lands!" exclaimed Grandmother.

"And the original sketch"—Grandfather fished in his vest pocket—"he's giving to our Derek, as a keepsake."

Derek took the paper. Yes, there was the DeWitt Clinton, the fuel wagon, the cars, and so lifelike he could almost smell the smoke and hear the captain's whistle. Beneath the picture, Mr. Brown had written *All Aboard!* and his name and Derek's.

"It's a wonderful keepsake!" Derek glanced at his grandparents. To his surprise, he saw that they were smiling, that they were not angry. "Would—would you care for me to describe the ride?" he queried timidly.

"Yes," said Grandmother.

"Do," said Grandfather, "because next time, *I'm* going."

"It was splendid," Derek began. "We went awfully fast. We went at a speed of *thirty miles an hour!"*

When a Modern Boy Travels

By Frances Cavanah

PETER WARREN lived on a California fruit ranch which his great-grandfather, John Warren, had bought in 1868. Peter liked to read the diary that his great-grandfather had kept of his journey from New York to California. It had taken John Warren three days to travel by railroad from New York to St. Joseph, Missouri, where the railroad ended. In St. Joseph he had boarded the Overland Mail, the line of Concord stage-coaches which carried passengers and mail to the Pacific Coast. That part of the journey had taken nearly a month.

Sometimes great-grandfather had traveled, not only all day but all night, sitting upright between two other passengers in the swaying coach. Sometimes he had spent the night in a log cabin along the way. A few times the other passengers wrapped themselves in their blankets and slept on the ground, while one of the men kept guard. This was in case Indians tried to attack them.

But the part of the diary that Peter liked best told how two highwaymen, wearing masks, had tried to hold up the stagecoach. The passengers then drew their revolvers, and began shooting through the windows of the coach. The driver laid his whip across the horses' flanks and they plunged ahead in a cloud of dust. Although the highwaymen had fired several shots, they finally turned back.

Peter always breathed a sigh of relief when he read that. For great-grandfather had been carrying the money with which he later bought the fruit ranch on which Peter lived. Peter started to keep a diary, too, but soon grew discouraged.

"I haven't anything to write about," he said. "Great-grandfather was always having adventures, but nothing much ever happens to me."

"No?" said his father, laying down his paper. "Well, I have to go to New York next week on business. Want to go with me?"

"Gee, Dad, when do we start?" asked Peter.

"Next Monday morning we'll take the bus to San Francisco. There we'll board one of the new streamline trains for Chicago. In Chicago we'll change to another 'crack' train. In three days we'll be in New York—a trip that took your great-grandfather four weeks."

The streamliner that Peter boarded in San Francisco was even more beautiful than he had expected. The silver-white locomotive and the cars behind it fitted closely together. Even the headlights were built into the engine. Nothing stuck out that might catch the wind and cause the train to slow down.

"Oh, boy!" said Peter to himself, as he followed his father down the aisle of a Pullman sleeping car.

On both sides of the aisle there were sections, with high partitions, or walls, in between. In each section two comfortable upholstered seats faced each other. The porter, the colored servant on the car, put their bags under the seats in the section where they were to ride.

Later, on the way to the observation car at the end of the train, Peter passed through other

Pullman cars. Some of these were made up entirely of compartments, or little private rooms. In the observation car people sat in comfortable chairs reading, listening to the radio, or looking through the big windows at the flying landscape. Peter sat down at a desk to write a letter to his mother. He had barely finished when a waiter came through the car.

"First call for dinner," he called.

On his way in to dinner, Peter had a brief glimpse of a small but complete kitchen at one end of the dining car. He sat down next to the window at one of the tables on either side of the center aisle, while his father wrote out their order.

"M—mm-mm!" said Peter when he had finally finished his dessert of ice cream and cake. "This beats great-grandfather's way of traveling."

Back again in their own section, they found that the porter had taken the cushions from the two seats and placed them in between the seats to make a regular bed. This lower berth, as it was called, was made up with mattresses and sheets and blankets. A shelf had been pulled down from the ceiling and made into another bed, or upper berth.

Green curtains hung before each berth, giving it the privacy of a little room. At one side there was a short ladder, and Peter climbed into the upper berth. Here he undressed and put his clothes in a little hammock hanging at one side. Crawling in between the cool, fresh sheets, he snapped the switch near his pillow that turned off the light.

Throb—throb—throb! The streamliner sped through the night over the shining rails at more than eighty miles an hour. But Peter was asleep.

In Chicago Peter and his father changed to a train pulled by a steam locomotive—a black giant of an engine—and by the next morning they were in New York. They took a taxicab from the station to their hotel. Peering through the window, Peter saw hundreds of other cabs, private automobiles, and trucks. Streetcars and buses crawled through busy streets and an "L," or elevated train, thundered overhead.

"But I haven't seen any subways, Dad," said Peter, as one of the elevators in the hotel shot them upward to the twenty-second floor. "I thought most people in New York rode subways."

"More than half of them do," said Mr. Warren. "We'll be riding in one ourselves, as soon as we get unpacked."

An hour later Peter was climbing down a stairway that led from the sidewalk to the station underneath the street. He dropped a nickel in a slot in a turnstile. The turnstile turned, and he and his father walked out on a long platform where a crowd of people waited. When their subway train came, the wide doors in the side slid open. Peter felt himself being pushed and shoved. Then he was on the train and it was tearing through a long black tunnel. Peter thought that this was a lot of fun.

But later in the day he decided that it was more thrilling to ride on a Fifth Avenue bus. From their seats on top of the bus, he and his father had a good view of the crowds of people hurrying along the sidewalks, the gay shop windows, and the tall, tall buildings. They left the bus near Rockefeller Center, where they went inside to visit the New York Museum of Science and Industry.

"I thought you'd like to see the travel exhibits," Peter's father explained. "Here are small models of a prairie schooner and a Colonial stagecoach and many other vehicles in which people used to ride."

What interested Peter even more was the miniature railroad exhibit. A small railroad had been laid out against a make-believe background of hills and trees. Mr. Warren turned on one of the five electric switches in the wall, and a tiny freight train ran along a track. Peter snapped on another switch. A streamliner raced along another track, dashing through a tunnel and speeding past miniature farmhouses, factories, schools, and churches.

"I don't see how people ever

went places before they had trains and automobiles," he said.

"They didn't go very many places, son," said Mr. Warren. "Sometimes people lived and died within a few miles of the houses where they had been born. Traveling was too hard and took too long. Even your great-grandfather was glad to settle down after his long, hard trip across the country."

Peter grinned, thinking of how he had traveled three thousand miles in just three days. "Wouldn't great-grandfather be surprised if he could read *my* diary," he said. Then he turned on a third switch and watched another little train whiz by.

From *Land Travel*